THE CLIFF PATH

Linda Newbery

Collins
An *Imprint of* HarperCollins*Publishers*

First published in Great Britain by Collins in 1995
Collins is an imprint of
HarperCollins*Publishers* Ltd,
77-85 Fulham Palace Road,
Hammersmith, London W6 8JB

1 3 5 7 9 8 6 4 2

Printed and bound in Great Britain
by HarperCollins Manufacturing Ltd, Glasgow

0 00 674765 5

Part One

We all leave home at eighteen or so in our family. Mum, to join the WAAFs during the war. Gran, so long ago that it's hard to believe it's still the same century, to be a nurse. Me, for far less creditable reasons. And now you.

In spite of everything it gives me a tug of nostalgia, seeing you packing; helping you to decide which things you might need, which to leave behind and which you can't do without. Sometimes our ages don't seem so very different, although at your age I did stupid things that you would never consider. I let people down; I hurt people I shouldn't have hurt. I was short-sighted, living in a dream world. But these are the last things I would have admitted at the time, least of all to myself.

I wonder how you'll feel when you look back? It's hard to imagine that you'll have regrets on the same scale as mine. You already seem so self-possessed, far more in control than I've ever been at any stage of my life.

That's why it's impossible for me to tell you more than the few facts you already know. I can't tell you how it was. I can't show you what it was like to be me.

* * * * *

Monday 1 July 1974

A good and bad day – started with a row and finished with a row. I'm so sick of my course! But the amazing piece of luck today was bumping into Paul and going to life class with him. It was fantastic!

"What a dreary place this is. Especially on a wet Monday." Abigail looked out of the rainwashed window as the bus pulled into the terminus with a swish of tyres on wet road. Umbrellas, raincoats, concrete and drizzle: you'd never guess this was supposed to be summer.

"What's up with you?" Lynne asked. "Bad weekend?"

Abigail pulled a face. "Had another row with my dad. Just because I got home late from a party."

Lynne shrugged, as if to say *Is that all?* The bus lurched to a halt and everyone began to file off: schoolchildren, office workers, early shoppers, all getting back into their weekday routine and looking as if they'd prefer to be somewhere else. The conductor was the only one who looked cheerful, beaming at the alighting passengers as if they were his dearest friends. Abigail didn't smile back. She jumped down and landed in a puddle, spraying dirty water over her own legs and those of a woman who was assembling a pushchair, with a whining infant in tow. The woman glared and tutted, but Abigail took no notice, stomping on to the pavement and looking down at the splash-marks on her bare legs.

"That's all I need," she said crossly to Lynne. "Both feet soaked and mud up my legs. Why can't they let us wear jeans?"

"Because we're supposed to look like secretaries," Lynne said mildly. "Here, come under my umbrella, and for goodness sake cheer up. Was it a bad row with your dad? You don't usually let it get you down."

"Oh, just him blowing his top about nothing at all." Abigail decided not to say that she had been at the party with Paul; he probably wouldn't want to know her after the doorstep scene in the early hours of Sunday morning. "He had a go at me for staying out late and not spending hours on my homework. Honestly, you'd think I was still at school. *Your* parents wouldn't have kicked up a fuss, would they?"

"No," Lynne said. "They'd think it was up to me whether I did the work or not."

Lynne would have done hers, of course. Abigail, who hadn't taken her shorthand books out of her bag since Friday's lesson, changed the subject by stopping outside Top Shop in the new precinct and pointing at a batik-print dress. "Look, that's nice. Couldn't afford it, though."

Lynne glanced at it briefly; it wasn't her style. "I keep thinking in shorthand, do you? Top – Shop." She drew the outlines on the window with her forefinger and flicked in the vowel sounds, light dashes for short "o".

"Can't say I do," Abigail said. Oh God, they were having a test this afternoon and she'd forgotten all about it. She would have to go over the exercise at lunchtime. Lynne would have done it last night and would be bound to get full marks; she could be irritating sometimes. Doing badly today would mean another withering look from Miss Spooner and a sarcastic reminder that a good secretary is always planning ahead, efficiently. Like Lynne. Lynne already looked the part, with her hair tied back in a bow, her neat court shoes and her briefcase containing all the files and notebooks she'd need today, with the pages neatly headed and dated. Abigail carried her stuff around in a shapeless tapestry bag whose lower stratum consisted of squashed chocolate bars, loose Tampax and crumpled pages of notes which should have been filed and learned. There would be enough time for being efficient when she got a job. For now, she was a student. She hoisted her bag more comfortably over her shoulder and adopted a slack-hipped saunter to distinguish herself from the office workers hurrying to their desks.

"Rachel's at home now, as well," she said, her thoughts reverting to the arguments at home. "Having Miss Brain of Britain in the family doesn't help much. Always there as a shining example. Why do I have to be lumbered with Goody Two-Shoes as a sister?"

"I thought you got on well with Rachel?" Lynne said.

"I do sometimes. But if only they'd stop going on about her all the time! *Rachel* didn't leave school at sixteen. *Rachel* always works hard for her exams. *Rachel* didn't argue with her teachers. And as for her place at Oxford, you'd think no one had ever done it before."

"Well, she did do awfully well, didn't she?" Lynne said.

Abigail humphed. Yes, Rachel had done well – three As in her A-levels. It had been what everyone expected, but it hadn't helped Abigail, especially when her own O-level results had turned out to be quite reasonable. "It's not too late to change your mind about leaving school,"

Mum had said. "I'm sure they'd take you back into the sixth form."

Abigail hadn't been interested. She had seen the last of school at the end of the exams and she didn't intend to change her mind just because of a few scraped passes and an A for Art. "Native wit, it must be," Dad had said. "Lord knows she did little enough work for them."

It wasn't as if she'd had much encouragement to stay on at school. Most of her teachers had shaken their heads doubtfully, making remarks about Willingness and Scholarship and Commitment. Lack of. Only Miss Clayton, who taught Art, had been enthusiastic, wanting Abigail to do Art A-level. None of the others sounded as if they could care less. They wanted to concentrate on girls like Rachel, girls who always did their homework and never ran in the corridors or forgot to change into their indoor shoes.

"You're much better off having an average moron for a brother, I can tell you," Abigail told Lynne. "OK, Rachel's brainy, but what good's a degree in Classics going to do her? At least we'll be able to get *jobs*."

"I know," Lynne said. "I'm going to do some temping in the summer holidays."

That was an idea. It hadn't occurred to Abigail that her typing skills might already be useful for earning money. She would need a job for a few weeks, and typing would pay better than waitressing or stacking supermarket shelves. She could save for some decent clothes, or a holiday – a real holiday, away from Mum and Dad. Lynne and her boyfriend were saving up to get engaged, which seemed a daft idea to Abigail. Settling for the first boy who came along showed a definite lack of adventurousness. Getting engaged was old-fashioned, and as for *saving up* for it – well, surely if you were planning it, then you *were* engaged? Lynne and Graham were already interested in the prices of semi-detached starter homes on the new estate. It sounded too safe and cosy for Abigail.

The college buildings were at the end of the shopping precinct, overlooking acres of London overspill housing. The campus was dominated by a glassy tower block that could be seen from miles away, even from the small market town six miles distant where Lynne and Abigail both lived. "A monstrosity," Abigail's mum called it. But then she thought the whole new town was a monstrosity, with its concrete and office blocks and brash new shops. "At least something *happens* there," Abigail argued. "At least there's a swimming-pool and a disco and a bowling-alley and a cinema. More than you could say for this backwater we live in."

Mum wasn't interested in discos or bowling-alleys. She only wanted peace and quiet, her family and her garden and her part-time job. She must have forgotten what it was like to be young. Admittedly the college buildings were ugly, but Abigail liked them better than her traditional girls' grammar school, with its names of long-dead ex-pupils carved on wooden panels in the entrance hall as if it were a war memorial, and its fossilized library where you had to creep around silently and try not to choke on the dust of centuries. It seemed to belong to the Dark Ages. All the other girls on the secretarial course, except Lynne, had been to the big local comprehensive. Abigail wished she had; they seemed to have had a lot more fun. All-girls' schools were unnatural, she considered; but there was time to make up for it now.

Lynne shook the raindrops from her umbrella as they reached the main door. Abigail glanced up at the clock and said, "Let's go down for a coffee before we go up to Typing."

"Hoping to bump into that art student?" Lynne teased, but followed.

The refectory was nearly empty. The serving-hatch was closed and a few students sat alone or in groups, with plastic cups from the automatic machine. Abigail didn't like the machine drinks, but she did like the idea of slipping in for a coffee before the day started. It was a reaction against years of school assembly, kneeling on the hard floor and droning out deadly hymns with batty old Miss Jacobs at the piano. Sipping coffee made her feel sophisticated.

Her glance automatically roved around for Paul, but he wasn't there; she hadn't really expected him to be. He was usually late. There seemed to be a different set of expectations for the art students: they could dress how they liked, they called their tutors by their first names and had free time to work on their projects. Abigail envied them; particularly now that she knew Paul, she wished she had taken Art after all.

"I haven't seen those two before," she said to Lynne as a pair of denim-and-leather clad engineering types walked through the refectory and out at the other end towards the Technical Block. "Perhaps they're doing day-release."

The taller of the two turned round to look, but Lynne wasn't interested in eyeing boys, being quite content with the unexciting Graham. She finished her coffee and stood up. "Come on. I don't want to be late. We're doing speed practice today."

She made it sound like a special treat. Abigail followed her back to the main foyer and up to the typing room on the first floor. Some of the other students had already started on their warm-up drills, and the room was full of the clatter of keys. Abigail sat down, heaved her typewriter out of the well of its wooden desk, and began on the warm-up. She didn't really mind the typing lessons, her fingers doing the work while her mind wandered elsewhere. She could type fairly quickly and her spelling was reasonably accurate, but tables of figures were her downfall, and that was what Miss Reeves chose to give them after the speed practice.

"*Blast!*" She slammed the carriage back and ripped her third attempt from the roller.

"What's the matter?" Lynne was working methodically at her task, a ruler marking the line she was copying. She never yanked her paper out or swore at her typewriter.

"You've still got twenty minutes," Miss Reeves' voice said behind her. "It really isn't difficult, not if you work out the spacing beforehand."

"I know *how* to do it," Abigail said. "It's just that it goes wrong every time."

"Try concentrating," Miss Reeves suggested crisply.

Abigail's weekend late nights were catching up with her. In the Office Practice lesson after break, she felt quite unable to take an interest in the relative merits of vertical and horizontal filing systems. Waves of drowsiness lapped at her brain. She would have to do something to avoid falling asleep on the desk. Opening her eyes wide, she tried to pay attention. Mrs Courtney, dressed in a smart pink suit, was holding out a cardboard file to show its plastic clip-tab.

"You can see all the labels at a glance, so when your boss asks for a particular file you can have it on his desk within moments," Mrs Courtney was saying.

Abigail stuck her hand up.

"Yes, Miss Fox?" Mrs Courtney raised her eyebrows, no doubt surprised that Abigail found the subject interesting enough to ask a question. She was the only teacher who called the girls by their surnames, as if this helped to create a businesslike atmosphere.

"Why do you always say *he* when you're talking about bosses? There are women bosses as well."

She hadn't really meant to sound rude but somehow the words had come out belligerently. One of the other girls giggled.

Mrs Courtney flushed slightly beneath her careful make-up. "Of course there are, but for ease of reference I tend to refer to male bosses and female secretaries, which is, after all, the case more often than not. I think you'll find that in the world of business, men do still outnumber women in positions of authority."

"It doesn't seem right," Abigail persisted. "Women are just as good as men at all sorts of things."

"You may well have a point," Mrs Courtney said, "but this isn't the time or place to discuss it."

"But," Abigail retorted, "it sometimes sounds like you're talking about the job of nanny rather than secretary. Get his coffee, bring him the newspapers, organize his train tickets, remind him of his wife's birthday, for goodness sake. I don't see why being a secretary should mean being a slave to some *man*. You'll be telling us next to wipe his—"

"Oh *really*, Miss Fox." Mrs Courtney gave a short laugh, of irritation rather than amusement. Lynne gave a shocked glance at Abigail, who muttered, "Nose, I was going to say."

"You seem to have forgotten," Mrs Courtney said sharply, "that you did choose to take a secretarial course, rather than a diploma in business management. And," she added, picking up another kind of file, "if you're planning to become a leading woman executive, I suggest that you try to grasp rather more than the bare minimum for your next test. Otherwise you may find there are better candidates for the secretarial posts you seem to despise so much."

Mondays weren't Abigail's favourite days, but this one was turning out particularly badly.

The drizzle lasted all day, and it was still raining dismally when Abigail and Lynne made their way back through the shopping precinct at half-past four. Abigail suddenly felt overcome with dreariness at the prospect of going home to face Mum's reproachful looks and Rachel's sisterly advice.

"I think I'll get the later bus," she told Lynne. "I want to look for some shoes."

They parted at the corner near the bus station and Abigail wandered aimlessly around the shops until they closed, rather bored but wanting to make her point by getting home late. Eventually she went into the public library; it was dry and comfortable in there and she could sit and look at books without anyone bothering her. She wandered towards the Art section and stopped with a shock of recognition as she rounded the corner by the outsize books. There he was. Paul. A little damp, as if he had just come in out of the rain. He was wearing faded jeans, soggy plimsolls and a purple T-shirt with the Andy Warhol design of Marilyn Monroe printed on the front. Abigail's first thought was that she could apologize for Saturday night; her second, that he might think she was following him around. Then he looked up and saw her, and grinned, without surprise. He was leafing through a book on Expressionism.

"They've got quite a good selection in here,"

he remarked, as though in mid-conversation. "What are you looking for?"

"Just browsing," Abigail said. She felt pleased to have bumped into him among the Art books. It fitted the impression she wanted to give of being misplaced in her secretarial course, more inclined towards the arts.

"Missed your bus?" Paul said, still flicking through the book.

"No. I didn't feel like going straight home. It's a bit tense just now. Parent trouble."

Paul closed the book and looked at her. "Still getting at you about Saturday, are they?"

Abigail nodded. "I'm sorry about all that." She wasn't sure how much to say, here in the library; you never knew who might be lurking behind the shelves.

Paul glanced at his watch and said, "Look, I'm just going to get something to eat. Want to come? I'm waiting for my life class. It's not worth going home in between."

"All right, why not?" Abigail said readily. She looked up at the library clock and mentally reviewed the bus timetable. She had already missed the second bus and would now miss the third as well, but that didn't matter. Paul left the Expressionism book on a table and they went out through the turnstile and stood in the doorway, looking out at the rain, which had intensified to a downpour. Abigail had a thin jacket on but Paul had no coat at all.

"Great! I love rain. Come on!" He grabbed her hand, leaped down the library steps and started to run, pulling her after him in a mad dash through the precinct. He was taller than she was, with a long stride; her tapestry bag walloped her as she lurched after him. Gasping, she followed him into the onion-smelling warmth of the burger bar near the cinema, and they slid into seats by the window. Abigail's hair had gone into corkscrew curls with the wet, dripping down the front of her jacket. She flicked the damp strands over her shoulders and smiled at Paul across the table, hoping she didn't look too much of a mess. She could hardly believe her luck: such a dreary Monday turning out like this!

"One thing about meeting your dad," Paul said, "is that now I know where you get that gorgeous hair from. Fox colour." He reached across the table and caught a strand of it and twirled it round his finger.

"I always hated it when I was a little kid," Abigail said. "Being called Ginger and Carrot-top and all that. But I quite like it now." She knew that her hair colour was eye-catching, especially now that she had grown it down past her shoulders and wore it loose. At school, she had always had to plait it or tie it back.

"You ought to," Paul said. "It's real

Pre-Raphaelite hair. Dante Gabriel Rossetti would have wanted to paint you."

She felt embarrassed by his attention, although she liked it. She said, "Dad's is a bit grey now, but that's the reason he's called Charlie – Charlie Fox, you know, like in fox-hunting. His real name's George, but no one ever calls him that, not even Mum. It's been Charlie Fox ever since he was in the RAF in the war. Stupid name, isn't it?"

Paul unfolded the menu. "What was he, a pilot?"

"No, an engineer," Abigail said disparagingly. "No Battle-of-Britain hero stuff for Dad. He had a safe ground job. That's how he met Mum – she was in the WAAF. What did your dad do in the war?"

"Nothing," Paul said. "He wasn't old enough. I'm having a hamburger – what do you want?"

"Yes, the same for me, with coffee." Abigail sighed. "That's the trouble with my mum and dad. There's such a generation gap. They didn't even have Rachel till Mum was nearly thirty, and Dad's four years older than her. They're too old to understand teenagers."

"Your Dad looked pretty alert when I saw him the other night, or rather morning, considering he'd just dragged himself out of bed."

"Oh, I didn't mean he's geriatric or anything.

He's got tons of energy," Abigail said. "It's a question of *attitude*. Who else's parents would have made such a fuss about getting in at three in the morning?"

"I suppose it was a bit late," Paul said. "I lost track of the time."

A sulky waitress arrived and propped herself against the formica table to take their order, and then Paul continued, "My parents couldn't give a damn where I am. They don't know, half the time."

Abigail couldn't decide whether his tone was wistful or matter-of-fact. Well, all right, she conceded to herself, her parents did *care* about her, but it was a bit stifling some of the time. A *lot* of the time.

"I'm sorry about the other night," she said. "Dad coming down and shouting at us. In his *pyjamas*. It was pointless trying to tell him we'd only been at your friends' flat. As far as he was concerned it was an all-night drugs orgy at the very least. I didn't think you'd want to know me after that."

"It's all right," Paul said. "I'm not put off as easily as that."

He looked at her steadily for a moment. The harsh lighting of the burger bar made him appear less good-looking than usual. He had thick hair, light brown, parted untidily in the middle and springing out into an unruly mass, darkened now with rain. He had grey-blue eyes and was quite tanned, to Abigail's envy; she often looked out of the typing-room window at the art students sketching in the sunshine. His expression could be stern but he had a sudden broad smile that transformed his face utterly. However, it wasn't only his looks that appealed to Abigail; it was the fact that he represented a way of life so different from hers. He was nineteen, he was on an Art Foundation course, he had his own car, he mixed with interesting creative people; most of all, he had an easy, casual approach to life which made nothing appear impossible or even difficult. And, Abigail thought, he likes me. He really likes me. It didn't matter that her feet were soaked and her hair was a messy tangle and she was on a tedious secretarial course; he had wanted her to come with him and he was giving her his sole attention.

The waitress arrived with a tray and plonked down hamburgers and cups of foamy coffee. The smell of crispy fried onions rose up, and Abigail started to eat, suddenly feeling ravenous.

"What about your mum?" Paul said, his mouth full. "Did she disapprove of me as well?"

"I expect so," Abigail said. "But her tactic is to make me feel guilty. She belongs to CND but she says she'd be quite happy with family disarmament."

"Belongs to CND?" Paul said, surprised. "I can't imagine my mum doing anything like that."

"My gran belongs as well," Abigail said.

"If your mum starts up a Campaign for Family Disarmament, I'll join," Paul said. "I've got three little sisters at home. That's why I didn't bother going home now. They'd be climbing all over me and wanting me to play games."

"That must get on your nerves," Abigail sympathized. She had no patience with young children. "What about this life class you were talking about? What time does it start?"

"Seven o'clock," Paul said. "You could come along too, if you like. I can lend you paper and stuff. Fancy giving it a try?"

"I suppose it didn't occur to you that your mother and I have been worried sick?"

It was a replay of the early hours of Sunday morning. Abigail caught in the front doorway as if she were a thief trying to break into her own home. Dad in the hall, stocky, outraged, like a bull whose territory she was invading. Abigail stared back at him, all the lovely excitement of the evening evaporating. They were all there: Mum looking anxious and relieved,

Rachel in the kitchen with a tea-towel in her hand. Trust Rachel to be doing something virtuous.

"You didn't need to worry," Abigail said. "I'm not a child. There's no need to send out search parties if I miss a couple of buses."

"But, Abby, it's gone *ten*." Mum was looking anxiously from Abigail to Dad and back again, her face strained. "Couldn't you have phoned?"

Abigail hated to see her looking like that, with little tired lines under her eyes. Mum could seem young, almost girlish sometimes, but in this light she looked middle-aged, with a lined face and hair going grey at the edges. Abigail felt a twinge of guilt for having been inconsiderate, but she wasn't going to admit it, not with Dad standing there waiting to triumph.

"I didn't think of it," Abigail said.

"No, you never do think," Charlie retorted. "That's your trouble. Never think of anyone but yourself. Mum's been on edge all evening. We all have. We were just about ready to call the police. All because you couldn't spare two minutes to make a phone call—"

Behind him, Rachel retreated tactfully into the kitchen.

"All right. You've made your point. Are we going to stand here all night, or can I come in?" Abigail dumped her bag on the floor and pushed past him to sling her jacket over the banisters.

"I suppose it's too much to expect an apology for spoiling our evening?" Dad said, with heavy underlining.

"Sorry," Abigail said gracelessly.

"I don't know what's got into you lately, Abby, I really don't. I'm not putting up with it. Treating the house as a hotel. No, worse than a hotel – you'd probably do hotel staff the courtesy of letting them know your plans . . ."

"All *right*, Dad. I said I'm sorry."

She climbed the stairs, half-expecting him to shout at her to come down again so that he could rant on for another ten minutes. But she heard Mum say quietly, "Leave it now, Charlie. I'll put the kettle on," and they both went into the kitchen.

Knowing she had been in the wrong didn't improve Abigail's mood. She kicked her shoes off and sat down on the floor and started brushing her hair. What had they been doing with their precious evening, anyway, that meant it had been totally ruined just because she wasn't there? You'd think they'd have been *pleased* not to have her around. Unless they *enjoyed* moaning . . .

There was a knock on the bedroom door and Rachel came in.

"What do you want?" Abigail said. "Come to have your two-pennyworth?"

"Actually," Rachel said, infuriatingly calm, "I came to tell you your supper's in the oven. Not that you deserve it."

"I don't want it." Abigail's response was automatic, but before the words were out she realized that she was hungry; the hamburger had been several hours ago.

Rachel sat down on the bed. "Look, don't make things worse. If I were you I'd go down and get your supper and say you're sorry for not letting them know. Dad hasn't been in long himself, he's been rehearsing, but they were awfully worried. They don't nag at you just for the fun of it."

"I wish they wouldn't treat me like a child." Abigail tipped her head and brushed her hair forward so that it covered her face.

"Then you shouldn't behave like one," Rachel said mildly.

"I don't mean to." Abigail realized that she did sound exactly like a sulky child. "When Dad starts on at me I just can't help it. He's so bad-tempered. I can't seem to do anything right."

"Dad, bad-tempered?" Rachel sounded so surprised that Abigail threw her hair back to look at her. "That isn't fair. Of course he isn't. And one thing you've got to admit is that he doesn't bear grudges. It'll all be forgotten about by the time you go down, and he'll be singing G and S as usual. He can't stand seeing you upset Mum, that's all."

Abigail threw the hairbrush into the clutter on her dressing-table and stood up, searching through her wardrobe for something to wear tomorrow; she was always in too much of a rush to think about it in the morning.

"You make me sound awful," she said resentfully.

Rachel didn't answer for a moment, and then she said, "Being away from home makes you appreciate your family. I bet you'll think that, one day."

"When I get the chance." Abigail hung a denim skirt and a yellow T-shirt at the front of her wardrobe. The secretarial students weren't supposed to wear denim, or T-shirts, but she didn't care. "You don't mean you prefer being here to being away at Oxford?"

"I don't prefer it, but I *enjoy* it. And by the way, I hope you're not planning to go on like this all summer. I've only been home three days and there've been three rows already."

"It's all right for you. They trust you. And you never want to do anything they'd complain about anyway."

"How do you know I don't?" Rachel said, amused.

Abigail looked at her. She was sitting on the bed with Abigail's old teddy bear on her lap, smoothing its patchy fur. Her hair was long, the same fox-red at Abigail's, but straighter; she was like their mother in build, small and delicate-featured. She was wearing jeans and a green cheesecloth smock, and her feet were bare. The way she was sitting, one leg dangling and the other curled underneath her, made Abigail suddenly want to draw her; her fingers itched to be holding a soft pencil, to sketch in the soft folds of the smock, the sweep of hair, the unconscious elegance of the pose. Her spirits lifted as she thought of the life class: the intense concentration on the model's pose, the sketch growing beneath her fingers, tentative lines turning into something three-dimensional and alive. Paul had been impressed, she could tell, even though he was doing something quite different, dark and scratchy. She could do it, she really could draw. She had almost forgotten what it felt like.

Rachel sat the bear on the pillow, and stood up and stretched. "Come on. Let's go down. I'll heat up your supper for you if you'll make a bit of an effort and tell Mum and Dad where you've been. Let's not go to bed with the atmosphere all prickly."

"All right, then." Abigail made a show of reluctance, but she recognized that Rachel's presence made it easier to get over arguments.

Rachel was a peacemaker, like Mum, but even better at it. And the unexpectedness of the outing with Paul had cast such a glow over the evening that even a row with Dad couldn't extinguish it.

Wednesday 3 July
Driving lesson with Dad.

"Dad said to tell you it'll have to be a short lesson today," Abigail's mother said, coming through from the kitchen with a basket of washing. "We've got to be round at the hall by six."

"OK." Abigail was waiting by the front window, flicking through her *19* magazine with one eye on the road outside. She had to admit that it was decent of Dad to fit in the driving lesson today, all things considered. Tonight was the first performance of *The Pirates of Penzance*, for which he was director and Mum was singing in the chorus, and it would have been easy enough for him to say there wasn't time to take her out driving.

She heard the jaunty beep of a car horn as the red Volkswagen slid past the window and stopped. She put on the glasses she had to wear for driving and called out, "Bye, Mum."

Her mother poked her head round the kitchen door. "Bye then, love. See if you can manage not to get each other annoyed."

Abigail grinned and went out. Oddly enough, she and her father never argued during the driving lessons, although they disagreed over practically everything else.

He had moved across into the passenger seat. "Sorry I'm late. Got stuck with a customer who couldn't make his mind up."

"Doesn't matter," she said, fastening her seat-belt.

The Volkswagen had trade plates on it as well as the L-plates; Abigail saw it on the forecourt of Fox Motors each morning, with a price on its windscreen, as she passed by on the bus. Soon it would be sold and she'd have to switch to something else. This was the third car she'd had lessons in. Her father said nothing while she got ready to start, but she knew he was watching to see that she did everything right: checking that the gear-stick was in neutral and the handbrake on; adjusting the driving mirror.

"We'll go along the High Street and then into the new estate," he said. "It'll be quiet enough there for three-point-turns and reversing."

Abigail pulled out carefully and drove along the quiet residential road to the junction by the primary school. She slid up through the gears smoothly, with a little flourish copied from Paul.

"How soon do you think I can put in for my test?" she asked.

"Not too far off," Charlie said. "But there's no point rushing it. And you'd better have some lessons with a proper instructor first."

"You're just as good as a proper instructor. Better." She found his presence in the passenger seat reassuring; he always seemed so calm, in spite of the scares she must have given him since they had progressed from the deserted airfield on to the public road. She couldn't imagine what it would be like with some stranger sitting there. Or, if she passed her test soon, with no one.

"No, you'll need a bit of polish," Charlie said. "I'm probably giving you bad habits."

"But driving lessons are expensive." Abigail knew how lucky she was to have her father to teach her; Lynne was having lessons with a driving school, and paying two pounds an hour for them. Abigail was determined to pass her test before Lynne did. She wondered whether her father was proposing to pay for the extra lessons, but didn't like to ask directly.

"How did it go last night, the dress rehearsal?" she asked.

"All right. Bit of a panic about the lights. Watch this idiot in the Cortina – he doesn't know which way he's going. I've got tickets for you and Rachel for Saturday night. Indicate right as you approach the roundabout – that's it, now left. Don't hesitate, you've got right of way. Rachel said that's what you agreed."

"OK. Thanks."

"Don't get so close to the car in front. If she stops suddenly you'll be straight in the boot."

It was just gone five. The High Street was at its busiest, full of shoppers, homecoming traffic, buses, bikes, and children dodging across the road. Abigail slowed to a careful crawl. There was so much to think about, driving; so many things to do with your hands all at once, and yet people who drove regularly seemed to do it without even thinking. When they had passed safely through all the potential hazards, Dad said, "I was thinking about the summer job you said you wanted."

"Oh yes?"

"You could work for me at the garage if you like. Then Mum could have a break."

"Oh—" Abigail was taken aback. "What, full-time, you mean?" Her mother only worked mornings.

"That's what I thought. You'd want full-time wages, wouldn't you? You could clear up the backlog of paperwork."

It wasn't what Abigail had imagined. She had thought of temping in London: a week here, a week there, in glamorous places like magazine offices or travel agencies.

"But I was thinking of working in London, in the West End," she pointed out.

"Go trailing all the way up to the West End?"

Her father sounded as amazed as if she had suggested commuting daily to the Outer Hebrides. "What on earth for? Spend two hours every day on the train, to say nothing of all the money you'd have to pay out in fares? Turn left here. Sounds crazy to me."

"No, it's not. They pay better rates for temping at the London agencies."

"But when there's a job waiting for you here?" Charlie looked at her and then shrugged. "Oh well. I won't try to talk you into it if you've got other plans."

He wouldn't understand. There was a world of difference between typing out car sales invoices in Dad's dreary little office behind the garage, and the London scene she imagined, where she would meet interesting people like fashion designers and journalists, and be invited out to clubs and bistros after work. At Dad's there was only Andy, the apprentice service engineer, who wasn't bad-looking at all and might even be interested in her. But Andy always wore greasy overalls and had filthy fingernails, and his idea of a night out was probably a game of darts at the local pub. No, she had better things in mind for the summer than Fox Motors. The whole idea was to get away from home and family, not to get more closely involved.

"Thanks for asking," she remembered to say.

Charlie said no more about it, and it was the nearest they came to arguing. She managed to get her five-point turns down to three, and only hit the kerb once when reversing round the corner, and then Charlie said it was time to get back.

"So you're going to carry on with those art classes, are you?" he remarked as she waited at the main road to pull out.

"Yes, it was great. I'm going every week till the end of term."

"Art always was your best subject. Good idea to keep it up if you've got the chance. OK, after this red Mini."

The drive home was straightforward from here on. He started humming one of the tunes from the show, drumming his fingers on his knee in rhythm. Abigail knew the song so well that she could have supplied the words: "*When the enterprising burglar's not a-burgling, not a-burgling, When the cut-throat isn't occupied in crime, pied in crime . . .*" He often accompanied himself on the piano, or sang at the top of his voice while he was doing the drying-up, with Mum joining in the chorus. In most families, Abigail thought ironically, the teenagers were accused of making all the noise; in the Fox household it was she who had to take refuge in her bedroom when she wanted to play records.

She parked outside the house, and her father broke off his humming and said, "Perhaps you take after your grandfather."

She looked at him in surprise. "How do you mean? I'm like *Grandad*? I can't see any resemblance."

"I don't mean him. I mean your other one. Mum's father."

Abigail often forgot that she must have had two grandfathers. The name Grandad brought to mind Charlie's dad, who was nearly eighty and lived in Leytonstone and had a liking for greyhound racing and Westerns. The other one, the Irish one she had never known, was a far more romantic figure.

She turned off the engine. "But how can you say I'm like him, when you've never met him?"

"Him being an artist," her father said.

Saturday 6 July

Went to see Gran at lunchtime. She showed me the paintings, all of them. It made me feel peculiar. Went to a party with Paul in the evening. I think he's quite keen! (And so am I.) Just my luck that it can't last long . . .

Abigail was fed up with her Saturday job at the baker's. Her feet always ached by the end of the day from the endless standing, and she had to wear a pink checked overall that clashed horribly with her hair. She had to be polite, serving customers with sliced whites and currant buns and bridge rolls, and she had to be sure she got their change right and didn't make a mistake with the till. At first she had liked having fresh cream doughnuts or éclairs with her coffee, but by now she couldn't look a cream cake in the face, and the other two women who worked there, Eileen and Connie, got on her nerves with their endless gossip about their families. It earned some money for clothes and for going out, but she didn't think she would stick it much longer. She could already imagine the scorn with which she would regard the cake-shop when she started temping, earning real money. And in the autumn, when she went back to college, she could probably find something more interesting if she looked; perhaps a Saturday job in a boutique, where she would get a discount on clothes.

As there wasn't much to do during her lunch hour, and it was too far to walk home and back, she often visited her grandmother: Granny Alice, as she and Rachel called her, to distinguish her from their other grandmother in Leytonstone. Granny Alice lived in a bungalow in a quiet close near the High Street, and Abigail often went round for a snack lunch, taking a French stick or some doughnuts or the spiced buns they both liked.

Granny Alice was seventy-eight but didn't look it. She was very like Kay, Abigail's mother, with the same small build, delicate features, grey eyes and wavy hair – except that Kay's hair was still soft brown with just a touch of grey, while Granny Alice's was nearly white. Abigail had the odd feeling that she was looking at her own mother as she would look in thirty years or so. Granny Alice lived alone, as she had done since Kay had left home to join the WAAFs and to work in Germany before getting married. Alice's own husband had died very young, shortly before Kay had been born. Abigail was newly curious about her grandfather. It had never before occurred to her to see any connection between her own drawing ability and her dead Irish grandfather, even though some of the paintings had always been displayed in Granny Alice's front room. In fact, there was one at home, in her parents' bedroom, a portrait of Alice in her mid-twenties. Because the paintings were so familiar, she had never looked at them properly; now she wanted to examine them closely, to see what kind of talent she might have inherited. If artistic talent *could* be inherited; she wasn't sure.

It was strange to bring the familiar pictures into focus, imagining someone working on them. There were three paintings and a drawing: two mountain landscapes, a sea view which

Alice said was Howth Head, near Dublin, and a pencil drawing of a tangled corner of a garden, which Abigail had always particularly liked. They were proficient enough, Abigail thought: a lot better than she could do, but a bit unadventurous.

"There are others, though, aren't there?" she asked.

Granny Alice nodded. "In my room. Do you want to see them?"

She led the way through to her bedroom. Abigail had rarely been inside; entering felt like invading her grandmother's privacy. There was a cream lace quilt on the bed, in the middle of which slept Granny Alice's large tabby cat. The furniture was dark and old-fashioned: a bedside table with several framed photographs on it, a dressing-table, a big wardrobe. On the wall opposite the window were two more paintings and several framed sketches. Abigail's gaze went straight to the self-portrait. It had an impressive bronze frame and a label as if it were in a proper art gallery: *Self-Portrait, Patrick Leary, 1896–1925.*

The style was bolder, more impressionistic than the landscapes. She had seen it before, but had merely looked on it as a picture of a man, as if she had no connection with it. Now, she thought, *This is my grandfather. This was*

Granny Alice's husband. Mum's father, even though she never knew him.

She felt a thrill of excitement, almost of recognition. It wasn't that she could see any physical resemblance to herself, nor even any likeness to her mother; more a sense that the person in the portrait was someone she could have met and talked to, someone who would understand her. The eyes were looking straight at her and the mouth seemed about to speak. It was a strong-boned face, with deep-set dark eyes and heavy brows, giving an expression of thoughtful intensity. An interesting face. He was young, not all that much older than herself. She remembered, and the dates confirmed it, that he had been only twenty-nine when he died. How odd for Granny Alice, she thought, to have lived with her memories for nearly fifty years. Hadn't she ever wanted to get married again? It seemed a terribly lonely life. And yet she always seemed content, even serene.

Granny Alice was looking at the other painting.

"*Roisin Dubh*," she said, as Abigail moved along beside her. "Dark Roisin, the spirit of Ireland. This was the last painting he did before he died. He thought it was his best. He was still finding his own style, you see."

Abigail looked. The painting showed a dark-haired, pale-skinned young woman against a shadowy background, with suggestions of mountains, hazy seashores and moorland. Looking closer, Abigail could see various figures in a swirl of activity, human and animal, as insubstantial as ghosts, forming a background from mythology. The large eyes of the woman in the foreground contained the same misty depths. It was a clever picture, Abigail thought, hinting at both calmness and turbulence. Perhaps that was how Patrick Leary had seen Ireland.

"It's wonderful," Abigail said. "This must be it, the style he was looking for. I wonder what he would have gone on to do."

Granny Alice said nothing for a few moments, gazing at the painting absorbed in her own thoughts. Then she remarked, "I was lucky to get it back. Did Mum or Charlie ever tell you about it? Patrick sold it, you see – he didn't want to, but we needed the money. He got a good price for it. He was just beginning to make his reputation – one of the Dublin galleries liked his work and would have taken more. We needed money quite desperately, because I was expecting the baby by then – your mum."

"So when did you get it back?"

"Not until after the war. Soon after Kay and Charlie got married, they decided to track it down. I still had all Patrick's papers. Your mum knew how much I wanted it, and she was determined to buy it back for me, even though she and Charlie had little enough money for themselves. So they went to Ireland. And by then the man who'd bought *Roisin Dubh* had died, and his daughter agreed to sell it. I don't think she liked it very much, but she still made them pay a lot for it. Probably more than it's worth, if you can put a price on something like that."

"It must have been odd for you, seeing it again after all those years."

"Yes, it was. Like having a piece of him back."

"Did you love him, Gran?"

"Oh yes," Alice said simply. "Though we had our disagreements, of course, like anyone else. We'd better have our lunch, hadn't we? Or you'll be late back."

They ate their salad and rolls outside, sitting on deckchairs in the small garden that smelled of lavender and geraniums. The sun warmed Abigail's face, relaxing her. She wished she didn't have to hurry back into town. She said, "What sort of things did you argue about, Gran?"

She would never have asked her mother that sort of question. *Do you love Dad? What do you and Dad argue about?* It was difficult to think of her own parents as having a relationship like other people's, or to think of them as young, falling in love, which presumably they must have done at some stage. Mum and Dad just *were*. But with Granny Alice it was different; almost as if there were less of a generation gap, rather than more.

"Well," Alice said, "there was Patrick's job. We argued about that, especially at first, when we went to live in Dublin just after we were married. His ambition was with his painting, not with his daytime job. But we needed money, of course, so we both worked. I was a waitress at Bewley's café and he took a mundane job in a bank. I thought he'd be bored with it, frustrated. I couldn't understand it at first. But he wanted a job that didn't tax him mentally, so that he could work on his paintings when he was at home."

Abigail thought of her grandmother, the pretty young woman she was in the painting, arguing with the young man who had been Patrick Leary. Did she mean really quarrelling, saying those bitter horrible things that Abigail so often found herself saying? She couldn't imagine it, not Gran. Abigail would have been embarrassed if Gran heard her saying half the things she flung at her parents. Sometimes she didn't even think; it was automatic, like Ilie Nastase slashing a forehand volley back over the net. Did *everyone* have such surprising depths of viciousness? She tried to imagine herself arguing with Paul, and failed. Paul had such an easy manner that it was difficult to imagine him quarrelling about anything. She almost opened her mouth to tell Granny Alice about Paul, but then stopped herself: he had made no arrangements to see her this weekend, to her intense disappointment. She hadn't even seen him since Monday. Perhaps he found her too dull, too conventional, with her safe, homely background? Perhaps she should have suggested something? With another boy she would have done, but with Paul, because it mattered to her, she lacked the confidence. She wished she knew how he really felt about her. He was maddeningly capricious, flattering her one moment, ignoring her the next, and yet she knew that this uncertainty was one of the things she liked about him.

"Even Pat's painting sometimes caused problems," Granny Alice said. "When he was really engrossed in a picture he'd work on it for hours at a time, hardly stopping for meals, and I used to feel that he hardly realized I was there."

Abigail flapped her hand at a wasp. "Did you mind?"

"At first, yes. It can be hard to live with someone who spends a lot of time completely absorbed in something you can't share. I felt left out. Until I accepted that his painting *was* him."

"And he did the portrait of you. That's beautiful."

"Yes." Granny Alice bent down to stroke the cat, which had followed them outside and was rubbing itself against her legs. "And gradually I realized that he was right to believe in himself. He was lucky, in a way."

"*Lucky?* To die at the age of twenty-nine?"

"Well, of course not that. I mean he was lucky to have found what he wanted to do in life, and to be succeeding at it."

"You know, Gran," Abigail said tentatively, "I'm beginning to think I should have done an art course after all."

When she got back to the shop, Connie said, "There was a phone call for you just now. Some chap."

"Who?"

"He didn't say. Just said he'd ring back later."

Paul. It must be! Suddenly cheered, Abigail put on her despised pink overall and took her place at the counter, ears straining for the phone. When it rang, she waited for Connie to go through to the store-room and answer it, not wanting to appear too eager.

"It's for you," Connie called.

Abigail went to the phone, not hurrying.

"Hi, it's Paul here. Your sister gave me the number. D'you want to come to a party tonight?"

She tried not to sound too excited. "Where? Whose? Oh God, I'm supposed to be going to my mum and dad's Gilbert and Sullivan thing."

"That sounds a bit of a drag. You can get out of it, can't you? We've been putting up the exhibition all day and Bill and Jess have invited us all round to their flat. It's an impromptu end-of-year bash. Go on, say you'll come."

"All right, thanks. What time shall I see you?"

"I'll pick you up at, say, half-past seven, then we can go to the pub first. And persuade your dad that you're old enough to stay out past midnight, will you?"

She giggled. "OK, I'll try." She rang off, excitement mixed with foreboding as she thought of explaining at home. They were bound to make a scene. Dad would view missing his Gilbert and Sullivan show as gross neglect of daughterly duty. Well, she told herself, it's Saturday night, and I'm old enough to do as I like. But by the time they had cashed up at the end of the day, she knew that she had no intention of explaining anything. There wasn't time. It was nearly six when she got home, and her parents were on their way out of the front door.

"Bye, love," her father said. "We'll see you afterwards. Rachel's got the tickets." Kay, following him with a bulging carrier bag in each hand, said, "She's watching Wimbledon. There's plenty of food in the fridge. The cheese flan needs eating up," and they were gone.

Oh, why did life have to be so complicated? Abigail wondered. If she'd *known* Paul was going to ask her out tonight, she could have seen *The Pirates of Penzance* on Thursday, with Gran. Fate had set itself against her, forcing her into trouble.

She sighed and went into the kitchen. Already hungry, she got herself some cheese flan and salad and took some in to Rachel, who was watching Chris Evert being interviewed about her Wimbledon victory. Abigail had been watching some of the tennis during the last fortnight, but there was no time now: she went upstairs for a bath, and prepared to take a good deal of trouble getting ready. She had decided to wear her black trousers, platform sandals and a new tunic she had bought in the Indian shop, dark green, with embroidery on the yoke and full sleeves gathered at the wrist. Wanting something extra, she went into her parents' bedroom and dabbed herself with her mother's *Je Reviens*. As she replaced the bottle on the dressing-table she saw her mother's heart-shaped locket lying there on the lace mat. That was odd – Mum always wore it, but perhaps she had had a quick shower before going out and had forgotten to put it back on. Abigail picked it up, idly turning it over in her hand, and noticed a small catch on one side. She prised it with her thumbnail and the locket sprang open to reveal a strand of dark glossy hair in the compartment inside. Intrigued, Abigail looked at it more closely. It wasn't Dad's hair, that was for sure, nor Gran's, nor her own or Rachel's. Why was Mum so attached to a locket with someone else's hair in it?

She heard the television click off in the room beneath her and then Rachel started to come upstairs. Not wanting to be caught examining Mum's private things, Abigail replaced the locket, darted into her own room and started to put on make-up. Rachel followed her in and sat down on the bed.

"You're going to a lot of trouble," she remarked, sprawling. "Are you trying to impress someone?"

Abigail searched for her mascara. "Yes, I am. But – look, Rache, you're going to have to make excuses for me. I'm not going to Mum and Dad's thing after all."

"Not going? Did you tell them?"

"I didn't get the chance. They were in a hurry to get there."

"So I'm going on my own now, am I? Nice of you to let me know."

"Well, if you haven't got anything better to do on a Saturday night . . . It won't make much difference to you, will it? I've been invited to a party."

Rachel sat up and buried her head in both hands. "Oh, God. I suppose that means another doorstep confrontation in the small hours. Just when I thought we were going to have a harmonious family Saturday night."

"They won't mind." Abigail shoved her mascara and eye-shadow into her shoulder bag and stood up, turning one way and then the other in front of the mirror so that the tunic flared over her hips.

"Yes, they will," Rachel said in resigned tones. "You know they will. What time are you coming home?"

Abigail looked at her. "I don't know, do I? Most people going out for the evening – most normal, adult people, that is – don't plan the exact time they're coming home, as if it's a railway timetable. I'll have to get a lift."

Rachel sighed heavily. "Where shall I say you've gone?"

"Out. With some friends from college." Abigail looked at her watch. "I'd better be going." She decided that she didn't want Paul to come to the house, not with Rachel there. She could walk up the road and wait for him at the corner. "Have a nice evening," she said cattily. "I hope you manage to stay awake. I'm not sure I would."

* * *

"No hurry," Paul said, as Abigail glanced at her watch. "There's no point getting there till nine-thirty at least."

"OK." Abigail tried to be nonchalant. Having been looking forward to the party all afternoon, she wasn't at all sure now that she wouldn't rather stay here in the pub garden. It was pleasantly relaxed, with long shadows on the grass and people in colourful summer clothes sitting at wooden tables or sprawling on the ground. She was pleased that Paul had brought her here instead of joining his other friends in a pre-party pub rendezvous. Quite apart from wanting Paul to herself, she couldn't help feeling daunted by the other art students. She knew most of them by sight but had hardly spoken to any of them, except Paul; they tended to stick together as a group, and she suspected that they thought of the secretarial students as dull and unadventurous, bashing away at their typewriters instead of struggling with the problems of self-expression. If it hadn't been for Paul asking her for change at the drinks machine and then dropping his money all over the floor so that they both had to grovel about for ages collecting it, she might never have got into conversation with him at all.

"So your course is finished now, with the exhibition?" she asked. "What will you be doing next?"

He took out a packet of cigarettes and offered her one. "I'm probably going to do a degree at Glasgow. At the College of Fine Art. It's one of the best places."

"Oh." Abigail tried to conceal her disappointment and to look suitably impressed. *Glasgow!* He could hardly be going much farther away. "No, I don't smoke, thanks. Have you definitely got a place?"

"More or less." He inhaled deeply. "I'll hear about it soon."

Abigail felt suddenly ashamed of her feeble efforts at the life class, good though she had thought them at the time. What had Paul really thought of her drawing? He must be exceptionally gifted, to be offered a place at Glasgow. She watched him smoking, his eyes narrowed against the evening sun as he smiled at her lazily. It didn't seem to occur to him that she might be disappointed by his going away.

"I suppose you won't know anyone else there tonight," he said.

"No. Only you."

He reached out for her hand and entwined his fingers through hers. "Don't worry. I'll look after you." His hand was firm and warm. "You'll like Bill and Jess," he continued. "Jess is a great laugh. I'm going to be spending the summer with them."

"You're moving into their flat?"

Paul laughed. "No. Wait till you see it – it's tiny. No, they're moving out. We're going down to Devon, renting a house from Bill's uncle. It's a place called Chilcombe Sands, on the south coast. Quite a few of us are going down. Sea, sand, sun . . . the chance to do some serious painting . . . get away from home . . . I can't wait."

"How soon are you going?" Abigail asked flatly.

"Next week some time. When the exhibition's over and they've packed their stuff."

Abigail looked at him, disappointment thudding in her stomach. He seemed quite unaware of how let-down she felt. Glasgow was bad enough, but this was even worse. Why was he bothering with her at all? Perhaps he was just using her to pass the time, the remaining days he had to spend grudgingly at home.

"Hey." He took hold of her chin and turned her face towards his. "Why so serious? You're meant to be enjoying yourself. This is better than sitting through those boring old amateur dramatics, isn't it?"

"You can say that again."

He laughed, and kissed her lightly on the lips. Then he fiddled with the neck of her tunic and said, "I like this green thing. You ought to wear green more often. It brings out the colour of your hair and eyes." He studied her for a moment as if she were an interesting composition, and then their eyes met and he smiled; Abigail hoped he couldn't read the muddle of her thoughts. When he looked at her like that, it was as if she were the only person who mattered, and yet he seemed totally oblivious of how she felt. It wasn't *fair*, she thought, the way he could send her spirits soaring one minute and crashing the next. She felt as if she were being swept along by something irresistible, unable to help herself, not sure if she even wanted to stop.

Dusk was beginning to fall, the pub garden illuminated by lights strung across the trees. Paul finished his drink and decided it was time to go, and they went out to his Mini van.

The party was in a tiny flat, more like a bedsit, in an unprepossessing council block. It was hot inside and the air was perfumed with incense or joss sticks. Discordant music played, something with an insistent pulsing rhythm that filled Abigail with vague excitement. Paul introduced her to some of his friends. For some reason she had expected Jess to be one of the beautiful girls, but Jess turned out to be someone she had seen around college, a dumpy girl with an unruly mass of hair, wearing jeans and a baggy denim shirt. She hardly glanced at Abigail, but started talking to Paul about someone they both knew. Bill, her boyfriend, had a round face and round spectacles which made him look comical, and wore a grandad shirt with red braces. He was friendlier, fetching Abigail a drink and introducing her to a bearded individual called Ollie, who was an incessant talker and backed Abigail slowly into a corner while he told her about the problems of transporting his paintings undamaged. Only half listening, and trying not to appear rude, Abigail attempted to edge back towards Paul, who didn't seem to have noticed she was being monopolized; he was talking to two attractive girls and making them laugh with some joke she couldn't hear. She gazed round at the bare white walls adorned with hangings of knotted string and beads. There was no furniture apart from a double bed on which five or six people were sprawling, and a number of floor cushions. By her feet a couple lay on the floor sharing a cigarette, each taking turns to put it between the other's lips, with devoted attention. Only one person was dancing to the music, a girl in a white vest and dirty jeans with a tasselled belt, who swayed gracefully and threw her arms and hair about, watched with bored interest by some of the others. Abigail felt self-conscious. It wasn't like any party she had been to before.

". . . and then I've been influenced a bit by Chagall," Ollie was telling her.

He was bound to find her out in a minute, and expose her as a keyboard-basher. "Is he the one with the floating cows?" she asked desperately.

At that point Paul came over, and said, "Don't bore her rigid, Ollie. Conversations are meant for two people, not one."

"She's not bored," Ollie said. "She's dazzled by my wit and intellect, like everyone else. See you later," he added to Abigail, and drifted off.

Paul put his arm round her shoulders. "Jesus, there's hardly room to move in here. Let's go outside for a bit, shall we?"

There was a grassy area outside the block of flats, sloping down to a shrubbery which led to the formal water gardens on the edge of the shopping precinct. The air was cool, not scented with flowers like the pub garden, but still refreshing after the clogged air inside. A few others were sitting by the fire escape; Abigail could see the glowing end of a cigarette, and someone was playing a guitar and singing in a waily voice. Instead of joining them, Paul took Abigail's hand and walked farther away, towards the dark shadows of the shrubbery. She could smell crushed grass and the sharp resinous scent of conifers. Paul sank to the grass and pulled her down beside him.

"Isn't it funny how you notice smells more at night?" she remarked.

"Mmm . . ." He buried his face in her hair. "Your perfume. It's delicious. What is it?"

"Oh, it's my mum's – *Je Reviens*. But I don't mean that. I meant grass and plants and things. Why is it you notice them more in the dark? I mean, they must smell like that all the time . . ."

Paul laid a finger on her lips. "Stop talking for a minute. You're as bad as Ollie." He kissed her, rather expertly, and then he lay back on the grass, pulling her with him. "Relax. What's the matter?"

"Nothing. Nothing's the matter."

He was laughing at her, teasing her. Her heart was pounding so strongly that she was sure he must be able to hear it. She wished it wasn't so obvious that he was the one in control, making all the moves. Other boys she'd been out with had been inexperienced fumblers by comparison. He made her feel like a gawky schoolgirl, far from the impression she wanted to create. She knew that he saw through her act of sophistication. And yet he didn't seem at all put off by her gaucheness; rather he seemed to like it, finding it amusing. His hands were inside her tunic, roving over her body.

"You know what I'd really like to do?" he said softly.

"What?"

He grinned. "I'd like to paint you. You're a

beautiful girl, Abby, do you know that? Can I? Will you pose for me?"

She felt enormously flattered. For an instant, *Roisin Dubh* came into her mind. Would he paint her like that: mysterious, remote, with unfathomable secrets? She imagined herself framed in a gallery, with critics saying, "Of course, this is the painting that first showed his mature style . . ."

"But how can you?" she said. "You're going away next week, aren't you? And then to Glasgow. We'll hardly have time to see each other again." Her voice was wavering, revealing her feelings all too obviously.

"There's all the time we want." He lifted a hand to stroke her cheek. "You didn't think I was going to clear off altogether, did you? Now I've met you?"

She was taken aback. That was exactly what she did think.

"But . . . you said . . ."

"Yes, I'm going to Devon. But that doesn't mean I don't want to see you any more. You've got all summer free as well. What are you planning to do?"

"Temping in London," she said without enthusiasm; the idea had lost its appeal.

"Aren't you going away?"

"I don't think so. Mum and Dad expect me to go to the north of Scotland for a fortnight. But their idea of fun is tramping through heather and staying in some damp cottage in the middle of a bog, miles from anywhere, with wet socks drying all over the place. I was going to stay at home, but they don't want me to stay there on my own."

"Come with me," he said.

She stared at him, but could not make out his expression in the semi-darkness. "What, stay at Bill's uncle's house, you mean? Are you serious?"

"Why not? They won't mind."

Her thoughts raced. "*They* might not, but my mum and dad would never let me go. They'd have fifty fits if I so much as asked."

"Ah yes." Paul lay back and linked his hands behind his head. "I keep forgetting what a good little girl you are."

Stung, she said, "Not all the time."

Abruptly, Paul sprang to his feet, and for a moment she thought he was so disgusted with her for her caution that he was going to abandon her and go back to the party. But he reached for her hand and pulled her up with him.

"Come on! Let's go for a swim."

"Swim, now? But the pool's closed and—"

He didn't answer, but dragging her with him started to run towards the shrubbery. "Paul, you're mad! Where are you going?"

She gasped, running awkwardly in her platform shoes.

"Going for a swim. I told you."

Twigs lashed Abigail's face as they plunged through the shrubbery and emerged at the concreted edges of the water gardens. The pool was a long narrow strip leading to a fountain at the shopping precinct end and bordered with formal flower beds. Paul let go of her hand, kicked off his shoes and unzipped his jeans. She watched him in astonishment. "You can't swim here! It's only about three feet deep! Anyway, you'll be arrested or something . . ."

"Oh come on, Abby. Aren't you going to come in?" Paul flung his jeans away and pulled off his T-shirt. His body was long and slim in the faint light, clad only in boxer shorts. She wondered whether he expected her to take her clothes off too.

"You *are* mad!"

"Yes, I know! But what's the point of being sane? Anyone can be sane." He leaped into the water, pranced about with flailing arms, and then lunged into a splashy crawl. Abigail thought his knees must be grazing the bottom. He rolled over on his back and shouted to her, "Come on! Don't just stand there! It's great!"

She dithered on the edge, and then he swam back to her and stood up and grabbed both her hands, and yanked her towards him. With a yell of indignation she plunged into the shock of cold water. As she grabbed at him he let himself collapse and they sank together into a swirl of water that closed icily over her head. Surfacing, Abigail disentangled her hair from around her face, gasping with shock. Her tunic, filled with air, floated around her like a child's water-wings.

"Oh, you—! Oh, my new clothes!" Hovering between anger and hilarity, she saw the ridiculousness of the situation. "You *are* mad! Totally, completely mad!" She grabbed at his head and shoved it under the water. It wasn't really cold after all, now that she was properly in. She groped for her shoes and threw them on to the paving.

"I told you you'd like it once you were in." Paul's arms tightened round her; she could feel the lean strength of his body against hers. "If you came to Devon with me, we could swim in the sea. Whenever we wanted."

"Oh yes. But why stop at Devon? Why not go to India or the Caribbean?" Abigail disentangled herself and floated on her back, gazing up at the sky. The moon was showing palely through wispy cloud. Paul's mood was infectious; if you could swim in your clothes in the water garden on a Saturday night, you could do anything you felt like doing . . . Why worry about parents and exams and qualifications? Paul never worried. Life was a party.

"You look like Ophelia, with your hair all loose and floating," he said, swimming close. "You know, in the Millais painting? I knew you were a Pre-Raphaelite. Stay there, just like that." She heard the splashing as he levered himself out of the water.

"Where are you going?" she said, dreamily.

"To get you some flowers."

She giggled and continued to float, imagining him picking daisies for her, crawling over the grass. He was idiotic, but she had never met anyone quite like him before. What would the others think, back at the party, when they appeared all wet and dripping? They would think she was as crazy as Paul. Perhaps she was, tonight. He had said she was beautiful and he wanted her to go away with him. What more could she want?

"Here, Ophelia." She heard the soft splash of something landing close by her in the water, and smelled the sharp aromatic scent of geraniums. Paul was standing on the edge, throwing flower after flower at her.

Sunday 7 July

Typical boring Sunday at home. Sunday lunch, washing-up, tea. Mum and Dad gardening and then dozing in deckchairs. Rachel acting as if she's already forty, quite happy doing nothing at home. I'm so fed up with it. Why do we have to go through the same tedious ritual, week after week? You'd think Sundays were sacred.

Mum and Dad were both in a mood and Rachel didn't help either. I thought I'd go screaming mad. If I could go away with Paul straight away, I would. Just to spite them.

They wouldn't even let me play my music.

The sun threw a stripe of sunshine between Abigail's not-quite-closed curtains and across her bedspread. She woke up slowly. The room was warmed by the sun, and she could hear a lawnmower outside. She groped for her watch: half-past eleven. She hadn't slept so late for ages.

Fragments of last night drifted pleasurably into her mind. Paul. The smell of geraniums. The limpid water floating over her body. Paul saying he wanted to paint her. Going back to the party, still clutching her geraniums, and exchanging her sodden clothes for a shirt and dungarees of Jess's. And then, less pleasant: coming home in the early hours, Paul's kisses in the car spoiled by the prospect of another doorstep interrogation.

And now she was fully awake, realizing that she still had to face it. There had been no confrontation; she had seen no one. The hall light had been left on but everyone was in bed and asleep. She had heard her father's snores resounding from her parents' bedroom as she tiptoed upstairs. God, she thought, how can Mum sleep with someone who sounds like an asthmatic pig? She managed to get in and out of the bathroom without provoking irate mutterings or irritable bed-creakings. She had written briefly in her diary, then lain awake in bed thinking about all the things Paul had said and done, while the sky had lightened to pale rose-grey and the first birds began to sing.

She knew that the row had only been deferred, not cancelled. She washed quickly, brushed her bedraggled hair and put on jeans and a T-shirt, and went downstairs. The kitchen smelled warmly of roasting meat. There were heaps of prepared vegetables on a chopping-board, and plates stacked ready to warm on the grill. Everything was quiet, apart from the lawn-mower outside. They were all out in the garden: her father mowing, Mum stooped and half-hidden by the overgrown plants in the border, Rachel busy with a rake. The perfect family Sunday, Abigail thought ironically, aware that the quiet scene would erupt into recriminations the moment she appeared.

It was too late to bother with breakfast. She sauntered out of the French windows into the sunshine and waited for her father to yell at her,

"What time did you come in this morning, young lady? Haven't we been through this enough times?"

But he said nothing, merely looked up and nodded as if she were a slight acquaintance, and carried on mowing. Mum straightened with a handful of weeds and said, "Oh, you're up," and Rachel said, "Good morning," with only the faintest edge of sarcasm.

Having geared herself up for a slanging match, Abigail felt almost disappointed. It would have been nice to stay out in the sunshine, but she couldn't just sit in a deckchair while they were all working. She went indoors and started flicking through the Sunday papers. After a while her mother came in and said, "Could you lay the table, Abby, please?" in a perfectly normal way, and went through to the kitchen.

It was the same at lunch. Dad came in from the garden to wash his hands at the kitchen sink, saying, "That smells good," as he always said, no matter what they were having. Rachel cooked the vegetables while Abigail carried the dishes through and Mum made gravy. Everyone behaved with perfect civility. It was completely unnatural.

Abigail ate her lunch in puzzled silence. What was the matter with them all? Had they forgotten about last night? Didn't they care that she had missed *The Pirates of Penzance* and had stayed out till nearly four in the morning? She would have liked to know how the performance had gone, but could hardly ask about it without drawing attention to her absence.

No one mentioned last night at all. Instead, her parents and Rachel discussed the holiday in Scotland: what maps they'd need to get, and whether they could get all the way to the north in one go or whether they should break the journey overnight. Abigail expected problems over whether or not she was going, but no one asked for her opinion. She began to feel like Banquo's ghost in *Macbeth*. Except that Banquo's ghost got considerably more attention.

"Abby and I'll do the washing-up, won't we, Abby?" Rachel said pointedly at the end of the meal, when their mother started to clear the dishes. "You two go and sit outside, and I'll bring you a cup of tea."

In the kitchen, Rachel ran hot water into the bowl and squirted washing-up liquid, taking no notice of Abigail and humming *I am the very model of a modern Major General*, a song from the production, one of irritating cheerfulness. Abigail picked up a tea-towel and stood resentfully by the draining-board. All right, if they were all going to freeze her out, she could give as good as she got. But soon curiosity overcame her resolve and she said to

Rachel, "Didn't they say anything about me not turning up?"

Rachel finished the phrase she was humming before replying. "No, not much."

"Didn't they mind, then?"

Rachel slid the apple-pie dish into the bowl. "Of course they minded. Wouldn't you have minded?"

"Did you explain? I asked you to—"

"Don't try to blame me. It wasn't just a question of explaining," Rachel retorted. "Can't you see it from their point of view? They've been working on this production for *months*, and you can't even be bothered to go and see it. Worse than that, you didn't even *tell* them. You just cleared off. It's not surprising they were disappointed, is it?"

"But I told you. I meant to go, if something else hadn't turned up . . . this party."

"Oh, yes. Something more important."

Abigail watched in silence while Rachel scrubbed at a bit of burnt pastry-crust. Well, the party *had* been more important. She didn't see why her parents should think they could lay claim to her Saturday nights. A sense of injustice overwhelmed her. There had been dozens of people at the party and it was a fair bet that none of them had had to go home to icily disapproving parents. It was underhand. Rows she could cope with, but this ostentatious avoidance of the subject was worse.

"I suppose,'" Rachel continued, "it hasn't occurred to you that you could *apologize*?"

"*Me* apologize? But they're the ones who've ignored me ever since I got up, making me feel like I'm invisible, or contagious."

Rachel closed her eyes exasperatedly. "All the same, if I were you I'd make them their tea and take it out and say you're sorry about last night."

"Oh, for God's sake, Rache. Do you *have* to be the perfect model sister, the adviser on good daughterly behaviour, *all* the time?"

Rachel shrugged. "Only trying to help."

"Keep it to yourself," Abigail retorted.

She had been planning to ask Rachel to sit for a sketch, but she was damned if she was going to now. She couldn't bear to look at Rachel's smug face any longer than she had to. All the same she made a pot of tea and put everything on the tray and went outside. One of the deck-chairs was empty; her mother had gone back to the weeding, while the other was occupied by her father who had fallen asleep with his mouth slightly open. He was wearing awful old corduroy trousers and a checked shirt with a frayed collar. Abigail rested the tea-tray on the low patio wall and looked down at him contemptuously for a moment, wondering why this scruffy man with greying hair and a middle-aged paunch should be able to intimidate and dominate her. Why on earth had Mum married him, when there must have been dozens of handsome pilots to choose from, in the war? Abigail had seen photographs and knew that her mother had been pretty enough, even in her WAAF uniform, to take her pick – especially in the air force, where there had been forty men to every woman. Surely there must have been more exciting alternatives, wartime equivalents of Paul, rather than squat boring specimens like her father? Was this what it all came down to – love, youth, romance, optimism, all dwindling into boring Sundays with the washing-up and the gardening? Abigail felt cramped by the Sunday ritual: the day revolving around the traditional lunch and the time-consuming domestic chores. She yearned to be somewhere else, doing something *real*. She pictured herself sitting on a cliff-top in Devon, painting something impressive, with Paul beside her. The vision made it all the more intolerable to be stuck here at home with the greasy saucepans and a snoring father.

"Thanks, Abby."

Abigail hadn't noticed her mother coming across the lawn. She turned rather guiltily.

"Wake up, Charlie." Kay nudged his elbow gently. "Abby's made us some tea."

His eyes opened, unfocused blue; his face

briefly expressed childlike bemusement. He looked vaguely at Abigail for a few seconds and then snapped awake, back into guarded disapproval.

Abigail poured his tea and handed it to him, and he took it with cold civility. Suddenly she couldn't bear this charade of politeness any more.

"Look," she burst out, "can't you say what you want to say? I'm fed up with you all ganging up on me."

Her father looked at her and then sipped his tea in an infuriatingly calm manner. "What exactly are you complaining about, Abigail?" he asked mildly.

That was a giveaway. He never called her Abigail unless he was really annoyed.

"You know what I mean," she retorted. "Ignoring me, treating me like an outcast. Why don't you have a moan, and let's get it over with?"

"Because," her father said with slow emphasis, "Kay and I have had an exhausting week, one way and another, and we'd quite like to spend a peaceful Sunday recovering."

Abigail felt slighted. If she wanted a row, then she was going to have it.

"I would have told you I couldn't go after all, last night," she said curtly, "only you didn't give me much chance, did you? You were in too much of a hurry. You didn't have time to stop and listen."

Her father only sighed, refusing to be drawn in.

"I don't see how you can make it our fault," Kay said. She was sitting on the patio wall with her mug of tea, looking up at Abigail with an expression that was difficult to read. "The point was that Dad had made sure to get you a good seat near the front, and the performance was completely sold out last night so that was a waste of a ticket. People were being turned away at the door."

"It wasn't the Royal Command Performance," Abigail said scathingly. "Only a little amateur do. It's not as though I've never been to one. They're all the same anyway."

"Leaving that aside," Kay continued more forcefully, "a mere matter of courtesy and consideration for other people, more important was that you didn't even let us know where you were. We had no idea where you'd gone, or who with, or how you were getting home . . ."

"I told Rachel I was going to a party." Abigail sat down in the spare deckchair. Standing in front of them felt too much like being sent to the headmistress to explain herself. "For God's sake, I'm not a baby! I got home all right, didn't I? What do you think I'm going to do, get lost and forget where I live?"

"There's no need to be rude to Mum," Charlie said sharply, sitting forward in his deckchair.

Abigail glared at them. "You just want to stop me having fun. You wouldn't care if I had no friends, if I stayed in every night. It's not fair! Everyone else is allowed to go to parties . . ." Anger was carrying her along like a strong current. She directed a new attack at her mother. "You left home when you were about my age. I bet you stayed out with all those airmen. Or did Granny phone the RAF every night to check you were safely tucked up in bed?"

Charlie put his mug down on the ground. "Abigail, I won't have you talk to Mum like that."

His voice was dangerously quiet. Abigail heard the warning note but plunged on recklessly. She thought of the golden locket with its strand of hair – Kay was wearing it now – and turned to her father in triumph. "It's *you* that doesn't like it. You don't like thinking about Mum's other boyfriends, do you?"

"You don't know what you're talking about," Charlie said, his veneer of calm giving way. "Anyway, we're discussing last night, not what might have happened thirty years ago. I won't have you upsetting Mum. Now why don't you go indoors."

It was an instruction, not a question. But before Abigail had time to decide whether she would lose more face by going or by staying, her mother spoke again.

"When I left home at eighteen, it was to do a responsible job in wartime. That meant being reliable, among other things. If I'd been as casual as you are about letting people down without notice, I'd have been kicked out of the WAAF in no time. God only knows what sort of secretary you're going to make, if you think you can disappear on a whim, and take offence every time someone asks you to do something—"

"I'm not going to be a secretary," Abigail muttered. "I'm sick of it. I hate my course."

Charlie threw his hands up and slumped back in his deckchair. "Oh, fine. So why are we supporting you through a two-year course?"

"*Supporting* me," Abigail retorted. "If only you did. You don't care about me at all! You don't care what I want. You only want a good return on your investment, don't you? Someone to do your dreary letters and filing at Fox Motors. Never mind that it's a tedious dead-end job that only someone like Mum would do. Never mind that I'd be bored out of my head." She didn't want to cry but her eyes were filling with tears of anger and self-pity. "You're not really interested in me at all! Just because I won't do exactly what you want—"

Her mother stood up.

"That's enough," she snapped. "We've heard enough. There's no point trying to discuss anything while you're in this frame of mind. You've had the satisfaction of spoiling our afternoon. Now go indoors and leave us alone."

Abigail recognized an uncrossable line when she saw one. She could not defy both of them. But she could still make her point. She stormed indoors, clumped upstairs to her room and slammed the door behind her. Taking out her portable record-player she put on *The Yes Album*, which she knew her father particularly hated, turned up the volume and opened the window.

Monday 8 July

Lynne's so boring. She doesn't understand at all.

I meant it when I told Mum and Dad I'm not going on with my course. All day at college I kept thinking, this is absolutely pointless. Who cares about the advantages of card index over microfiche? I'm beginning to feel as if my brain is a filing system, full of useless information.

Mum and Dad have grounded me but I'm not taking any notice. I'm going to the exhibition with Paul tomorrow night. If I don't see him I'll go mad.

* * *

"I'm in love," Abigail said on the bus.

"Oh yes?" Lynne sounded sceptical rather than impressed. "And exactly how long have you known this dream man of yours?"

"A few weeks. It's not *time* that matters," Abigail said scathingly, "not when two people are as obviously right for each other as Paul and I are. I mean, we both just *know*."

"He loves you too, does he?" Lynne said.

God, she was so literal-minded. "Yes, he does," Abigail said airily.

"How do you know?" Lynne pursued, like a terrier after a rat. "Has he said so?"

"Well, of course he has – as good as said so." Abigail felt irritated. There was no way of conveying to Lynne the intoxicating excitement of being with Paul. Lynne was probably jealous, because Paul was so much more desirable than boring old Graham. "He hasn't offered me an engagement ring, or suggested we start saving up for a mortgage, if that's what you mean," she said snidely. "He's an artist. He's unconventional. We had such a great time at the party on Saturday night. We swam in the water gardens and then he picked me a bunch of geraniums and said I was like Ophelia."

Lynne's neat eyebrows shot up under her fringe. "Swam in the *water gardens*? He sounds like a bit of a loony. And do you mean to say you took your clothes off?"

"No, I didn't. He's spontaneous, unpredictable, if that's what you mean by loony," Abigail corrected. "There's nothing wrong with that. That's what I like about him. You never know what's going to happen next."

"And Ophelia? Isn't she one of the swans in *Swan Lake*? Can't see much of a resemblance myself."

"No, she's in *Hamlet*, you moron. He meant," Abigail said loftily, "that I looked like the Pre-Raphaelite painting by Millais."

"He sounds a bit of an intellectual," Lynne said doubtfully. "Anyway, about these geraniums. Where did he pick them from?"

"You do ask some weird questions. From the flowerbeds in the water gardens, of course. What on earth do you want to know that for?"

"Because," Lynne said with severity, "my uncle works as a council gardener. He probably planted those same geraniums. And who pays for them? The tax-payer, that's who. Paul's got no business picking them."

"Oh, for goodness sake, Lynne." Abigail got to her feet as the bus pulled in. "I'm only talking about a few geraniums, not the whole municipal planting scheme. There's no romance in your soul, is there?"

Tuesday 9 July

It's decided now. But I'd better not write any

more in case someone reads this. You never know who might come prying in my room while I'm out.

Between college and the opening of the exhibition at seven o'clock, Abigail went for a drink with Paul in a bland modern pub on the edge of the shopping centre. The bar was almost empty at this time of the evening. Thinking that she was more likely to be challenged for being under-age now than when there were other drinkers to divert the landlord's attention, Abigail asked for lemonade and lime, but Paul told her not to be silly and ordered lager.

"Don't *worry* about everything. You're not going to get into trouble."

She smiled. "I'll be in trouble all right. My Dad's said I'm not to go out in the evening for the next two weeks. Honestly, I've just about had it up to here. You'd think my Dad lived in Victorian times, the way he goes on. I've told them I'm packing in my secretarial course but they're insisting I carry on."

"Did you mean it the other night when you said you'd come down to Chilcombe? That would be a way out."

Abigail couldn't remember exactly what she had said, or what she had meant to say, but she replied, "I'm definitely not going to Scotland, that's for sure. They'd never agree to me going away with you, not in a million years. But I think I'll come anyway."

"Terrific! As long as they don't come hammering on the door accusing me of white slave trafficking."

Abigail wasn't sure of the implications of that, but the vision of her parents setting off in outraged pursuit was only too convincing. She said, "They won't be able to, if I don't tell them where I'm going."

Paul smiled approvingly. "You're getting quite rebellious, aren't you?"

"A case of having to, with parents like mine."

"They sound like my folks," Paul said. "Wrapped up in their own petty lives. As long as they've got their cosy little home and a car parked outside and money in the bank, they don't care about anything else. I mean, Vietnam might have been happening on another planet for all it meant to them, and the miners were just a lot of troublemakers out for what they could get. Look after number one, that's their motto. It makes me sick. I couldn't stick it at home any longer than I have to."

"That's exactly how I feel about mine," Abigail said. She tried to think of something she ought to be outraged about to show that she wasn't complacent like her parents and Paul's, but could only think of the Watergate scandal and was not sure what opinion she ought to have on it. "They're just the same," she finished lamely.

"There you are then. Good reason for getting away. Show them you can be independent."

She watched him rolling and unrolling an empty crisp packet. He had very long thin fingers, like twigs. Artist's hands, she thought. A smudge of paint on a thumbnail, a skinned patch over one of the knuckles. Sensitive hands that knew how to rove over her body, exploring. Paul had been fairly restrained so far, in deference perhaps to the inexperience which she could not conceal, but when she went away with him there would be no more restraint. He looked up at her and smiled, as if knowing what she was thinking, but all he said was, "Drink up. It's time I got back."

They finished their drinks and walked back to college. Abigail half-wished she hadn't stated her intention so openly; now that she'd said it, it would be difficult to back down. Yet for the same reason she was glad she *had* agreed. It was beginning to seem real. She imagined a cottage in a picturesque village sheltering between cliffs; there would be a fishing harbour, perhaps a pub and a tea-shop or two. Fishermen bringing in their catch, with gulls wheeling. Herself with Paul, walking along the sand in the moonlight, holding hands, their bare feet trailing through the waves. She thought of the portrait he would paint of her. He would make her look beautiful, and everyone who saw it would know how he felt about her.

The art rooms were long raftered buildings with enormous windows along both sides. Abigail had often looked across from the typing room on the opposite side of the paved garden, envying the art students their freedom and self-expression, while she scrubbed at a mistake on her carbon copy. Since the party, and because she was with Paul and they were planning to escape together, she was beginning to feel that she inhabited the edges of their world, and could no longer be regarded as a separate species concerned only with dingy offices and invoices. The paintings and sculptures displayed on screens and tables made her feel more strongly than ever that she should have taken an art course. She thought disparagingly of the results of her own three terms at college – a Stage 1 Typing Certificate, a none-too-accurate command of shorthand, and a nodding acquaintance with various filing systems. It had been a process of stifling and narrowing rather than expansion. Why had she ever wanted to do it?

There was wine and fruit juice to drink, and soft guitar music playing. Most of the girls had dressed for the occasion in long cheesecloth dresses and beads, or floaty tunics. Jess, though, was dressed exactly as before, in denims and a man's checked shirt, and her hair stood out in a wild tangle. Abigail had almost forgotten about Jess when thinking about her flight to Devon; Jess didn't quite fit in with the soft-focus vision of dreamy contentment. She had imagined herself alone with Paul, but of course there would be lots of other people at the house; Paul had said so.

"Thanks for lending me the clothes the other night," Abigail said. "They're in Paul's van."

"That's OK," Jess said, frowning at a wall full of screen prints.

"Abby's coming down to Devon for a couple of weeks," Paul told her. "That's all right, isn't it?"

"Sure. Bring who you like," Jess said.

"These are Jess's prints," Paul said to Abigail. "Brilliant, aren't they?"

"Yes," Abigail said lamely. The prints showed enormous suns, or stars perhaps, in deep colours which melted into each other and blurred before her eyes.

Jess looked at Abigail for the first time. "He's only saying that so I'll have to say his paintings are brilliant too," she said. "Have you seen them yet?"

"No, where are they?"

"I'll show you," Paul said.

The need to respond appropriately made Abigail feel anxious. She stood in front of the six big framed paintings. They were all similar – thick black gashes against backgrounds of grey and smoky blue. She wondered now what she had expected. People didn't do conventional landscapes and still lifes any more, not if they were art students. They worked in more experimental styles. And she had seen Paul's dark scribbly style of drawing at the life class. What had he really thought of her own tentative efforts? She frowned intently at the canvases, sure that they would tell her something about Paul if she could only understand.

"They look angry," she said eventually.

Paul smiled. She had evidently said the right thing. "Good. They're supposed to be angry."

"Angry about what?"

"Everything. Life. Hypocrisy. The establishment."

She was surprised. Paul didn't strike her as an angry person: relaxed, laid-back, she would have said. Perhaps his anger went deeper than her own short-lived fireworks. He needed his painting to express his feelings. And he must be good, if he was going to Glasgow.

"Which do you like best?" Paul asked.

Abigail considered carefully before pointing to one which had a sprinkling of white blobs over the dark colours, as if a loaded paintbrush had been flicked at it; she thought it less gloomy than the others. Paul nodded slowly, to her relief. It was dangerous ground, she felt, where a wrong choice or unappreciative comment could reveal serious personality defects.

They moved on, and Paul waved a dismissive hand at the graphic design section. "That's just commercial stuff. This is more interesting." He led her towards the sculptures, mainly assemblages of metallic junk or bits of bent stripped wood. Abigail was completely out of her depth here, unsure how you could tell what was good and what wasn't. When she asked Paul, he said that was an over-simplistic way of looking at it.

"Have you got much preparation to do over the holidays?" she asked him.

He looked at her blankly, and she explained, "For the course at Glasgow."

"Oh . . . no, not really." He lowered his voice. "Look, you'd better not mention Glasgow here tonight. One or two of the others wanted to go there and couldn't get places. And the fact is, I might not go to Glasgow after all, not straight away. I'm thinking of taking a year out."

"Why?" Abigail couldn't resist thinking that it might be because he didn't want to leave her.

"Oh, various reasons." Paul smiled at her. "Especially now that you're coming with me."

"But that's only for—"

"Listen." He moved closer, taking her arm. "I'm thinking of staying on at Chilcombe Sands. Get some casual work or pitch in with Bill and Jess. There are loads of galleries down there and I'd like to see if I can sell some of my work. Why don't you come too? I mean, not just for a week or two – why don't you chuck it all in, leave home for good? You don't have to do an art course to be an artist. You just do it. You've got just as much talent as half this lot. Why not have a go?"

"Leave home for good?" The sheer madness of the idea appealed to her. "But how could I?"

He shrugged. "People do. It's easy enough. Just get on a train and go. You don't have to tell anyone, like you said."

"But what about money?"

"No problem. It's a holiday resort. There are loads of jobs, especially in the summer. We can get casual work."

"And what about Glasgow?"

"Don't worry about that," Paul said off-handedly. "That's ages away. There's no point in trying to plan too far ahead. If it works out, we'll think of something. Get a place of our own."

"Do you mean it?" she said, suddenly fired up with excitement.

"Of course I mean it. Why not?"

Abigail knew that her parents would have suggested a hundred and fifty reasons why not, but Paul looked at her with his sudden intimate smile, and none of them seemed in the least important.

Part Two

I can still remember, quite clearly, how I felt about leaving. There was a sort of triumph, because I thought I'd finally shown them, my mum and dad, that I didn't have to let them run my life for me; I could do without them. I was much given to dramatic gestures at that time of my life and this was the most dramatic exit I'd ever made. I didn't know that that sort of triumph is always hollow, because of course you're not there to see the impact you've made; you can only imagine.

And if I *had* been there to see the effect on my parents, it wouldn't have been triumph at all. I think I must have known that, even then. I thought I'd never see them again. It seemed as final as that. I'd taken an irrevocable step – thrown everything back in their faces.

I was on the train but I was nowhere. I'd left

my past life behind me but I hadn't got a new one yet. Once I'd got away, I remember feeling such a sense of freedom – as if I could go anywhere, do anything, become anyone. I thought I'd left all the bad things in my life behind and from now on there would be only fun and excitement. It was going to be a new life, and I expected to have a new self, to start it with.

* * * * *

Monday 15 July

I'm writing this on the train. Paul's been gone since Friday, with the van and most of the stuff we're taking. It was odd, packing, not just for a holiday but for ever, knowing that I'll never go home again and whatever I've left behind I've left for good. I feel a bit mean about not telling Lynne, but then she would have been bound to tell Mum and Dad if they asked her. Perhaps I'll send her a postcard some time.

It's half-past eleven. I keep looking at my watch and wondering what they're doing at college. Speed practice at the moment I suppose. I can forget all that – it doesn't matter any more.

Even though I couldn't wait to leave home, it

was a bit sad when it came to it. All the secrecy over the last week sort of took over, so it was only when I got out of the house that I finally realized what I was doing. I almost ran back indoors, but then I thought of Paul waiting at Chilcombe station and of course I had to go. And anyway I haven't got a key any more. I left that behind.

It took some planning. I kept thinking that Mum or Rachel would come into my room and see how much was missing – all the stuff I smuggled out to Paul on Friday. I had to pretend I was ill this morning. Rachel was going to meet a friend in London and she took so long leaving that I nearly had a nervous breakdown, waiting. And then I was afraid I'd meet her on the Underground before I got to Paddington.

But that's all over now. I'm on my way.

I didn't think of bringing a book to read. Now I've got nothing to do except write this. I hope the man opposite can't read upside down.

I keep wondering when they'll first realize. Mum probably won't notice anything when she gets in at lunchtime. I won't be on the usual bus home, but that's happened enough times before. Eventually I suppose someone will go into my room and notice what's gone. I'll just have to hope they don't report me to the police or anything like that.

Perhaps I should have left a note. I thought of

it, but I didn't know what to say. It would have seemed a bit like committing suicide.

Worst of all was nearly going to see Granny Alice yesterday and then deciding not to. I wanted to see her one last time but I was afraid I'd find myself telling her all about it. She doesn't know anything about my rows with Mum and Dad (unless they've told her). I get on far better with her than with either of them.

I mean *got* on better. That's in the past now.

Now I'm going to start my new life. I feel excited but a bit frightened as well. *Everything's* going to be different.

After Exeter, the railway line ran close to a wide river estuary, which spread out into shining mud-flats and calm waters like a map of freedom. Abigail stared out at the enticing distances, her spirits lifting; this was why she had come. *It will be all right, it will be all right*, a voice sang in her head. She felt like a child going on holiday, making up chants to the train's rhythm. *Paul will be there; it will be all right.*

She had looked up Chilcombe Sands in her parents' road atlas at home. It was a spreading splodge on the map: quite a large town, not the picture-postcard fishing village she had imagined at first. Paul had said it was a tourist resort. That was better, really, because they would need jobs. It would be hard to find work in a fishing village, but in Chilcombe Sands there would be pubs, cafés, hotels, holiday camps; perhaps she could even find a job in an art gallery. Typing would pay better, but she didn't think that would be in keeping with her new way of life. She was going to be an artist now. She had left her smart secretarial skirts and blouses behind, and brought only the clothes she liked best.

The train was slowing. She pulled her bags down from the rack and got off with several other passengers who marshalled small children and lugged suitcases. It made her think of a family holiday in Devon once, near Bideford; they had stayed on a farm where Rachel had been frightened of the cows and Mum had slipped over in a patch of dung . . . But she wasn't going to think about that now. She turned her thoughts to the next few moments, suddenly panic-stricken in case Paul wasn't there to meet her. Maybe he had changed his mind, and didn't want her? What would she do then, alone in this strange place with nowhere to go?

She hurried through the barrier and scanned the ticket hall anxiously. There he was, leaning against the wall by the main doors, his hair wind-blown. He grinned and came towards her, and she dropped her bags and flung herself into his arms, dizzy with relief.

"Hey, steady on. What's the matter?"

"Oh God. We've done it. We've actually done it." She had a faceful of his hair and purple T-shirt, smelling his familiar smell. Her arms tightened round him. "I still can't believe it. I feel as if I've escaped from Colditz."

"Daft girl!" He kissed her quickly. "Come on, let's go. The van's outside."

They carried the bags out to the station car park, Abigail looking around for glimpses of her new life. The station was at one end of a long High Street, with all the usual shops: Boots, Woolworth, the Co-op, just like home. No seafront; only the wheeling cry of a gull overhead indicated its nearness. Abigail sniffed for salt wind but could smell only car fumes. It was early evening; a shopkeeper dragged a postcard stand through a doorway, someone else was pulling down blinds. A couple dressed alike in shorts and flip-flop sandals looked in a tea-shop window.

"Which way's the sea?" Abigail asked as they stowed the luggage in the back of the van.

Paul grinned, getting into the driver's seat. "You're like a little kid, aren't you? I bet you've brought your bucket and spade."

"I've never lived near the sea before," she protested.

Paul started up and looked over his shoulder before reversing. "Only joking. I'll drive you along the front before we go to the house. We can have a better look round later."

The narrow streets closed in as if guarding a secret and then, as if it could be hidden no longer, parted to reveal the wide expanse of the coastline. Calm grey-blue sea, fenced by a railed promenade; ice-cream vans, an attendant stacking deckchairs, rows of parked cars. Along the seafront, the styles of several different eras struggled for supremacy. Elegant Victorian hotels with impressive steps and awnings faced the sea for a short stretch, then gave way to beach cafés and amusement arcades. In the other direction a harbour wall reached out like a bent elbow, cradling a forest of masts; beyond was a glimpse of a wide estuary with grass-topped cliffs on the other side.

"Isn't the house by the sea?" she asked as Paul steered away from the harbour. He seemed to be heading back towards the station.

"It's a few minutes' walk. Just along here. Princeton Terrace."

They turned into a residential street of narrow terraced houses, each with a small front garden. Paul parked by the roadside and said, "This is it. With the red front door."

Abigail got out of the van and looked at her new home. It was solidly-built, whether Victorian or Edwardian she wasn't sure. It had a bay window overlooking a messy garden of dandelions and nettles, sandwiched between its two neat neighbours like a tramp between wedding guests. There was a sort of tunnel or alleyway through to the back, housing overflowing dustbins. The front door, newly-painted in aggressive pillar-box red, was the only sign that the house had received recent attention. The door had a glass panel with a tulip pattern in stained glass, above which was the number 32; one of the screws which should have supported the 2 was missing, so that it swung at an angle. This was her new address: 32 Princeton Terrace, Chilcombe Sands, Devon. This was going to be home.

"Will anyone be in?" she asked, rather hoping not. She wanted to install herself before meeting Bill and Jess and the others.

"No idea. We all come and go."

Paul glanced up at the top floor as he spoke. Following his gaze, Abigail saw closed curtains at a dormer window.

"How many people are staying here?"

"Six, counting you. At the moment. Ollie and some of the others are coming down later. There's Bill and Jess, Gillian who lives up at the top, and a bloke called Beano."

"Beano? You're joking!"

"I'm not. That's all he ever reads, that and the *Socialist Worker*, which he sells in town every Saturday." Paul passed her the bags and locked up the van, and put the keys into his jeans pocket, getting out a more substantial one on a fob. Abigail followed him up the steps and into the house.

It was quite spacious inside. There was a proper hall, and a big front room leading off it.

"People paint and work in here," Paul said, in the main room. "Except Gillian. She does all hers upstairs."

There was a clutter of cardboard boxes, paint-stained jam jars and tubes of paint in one corner, a record-player and stack of records in another. No furniture apart from one paint-splashed stool at an easel, and some floor cushions. There seemed to be no one about, but Abigail could hear music coming from upstairs.

"Dining room through here," Paul said. "Very posh we are. Although it's difficult to dine in the dining room, or anywhere else come to that, because there's no table to dine off. At least we've got plates. Kitchen this way—" He opened another door. "There's an enormous pantry-thing through here. Sink full of washing-up, as usual. We always argue about who ought to do it, so no one does."

He led the way upstairs. There was no carpet on the stairs, just bare boards, and faded lino on the landing. A narrower flight of steps led up to the top floor.

"Bog here, bathroom next door. This is a

spare room till Ollie comes, full of junk. That's Bill and Jess's room. The one at the front's ours."

Ours. Our room. Abigail hadn't quite expected this, although she knew it would sound incredibly foolish to say so. She had vaguely imagined some sort of communal sleeping arrangement, the kind of thing that happened after parties. Sleeping with Paul was going to happen at some stage, she had accepted that by coming away with him, but now that it was going to happen here, tonight, she felt unaccountably daunted. She looked at the double mattress on the floor.

"I didn't think we'd have a room of our own," she said.

"It's great, isn't it?" Paul said, not noticing her doubtful tone. He took the bag from her and then put his arms around her and nuzzled his face into her hair.

She pulled back slightly. "Look, I— I—" She didn't know how to put it.

"What?" He looked at her, amused, tolerant. Perhaps he did know, after all.

"I— I'm not on the Pill, or anything. I mean, it all happened so quickly, deciding to come away – there wasn't time to go to the doctor or anything like that."

"That's all right," Paul said, unconcerned. "We can sort that out later. I got some johnnies in case you hadn't had time to get yourself fixed up."

He made it sound like getting a car serviced, no more significant than that, but no more daunting either. Abigail wondered briefly how many other girls had got themselves *fixed up* for Paul, and then reassured herself that at least he knew what it was all about. She detached herself from him and looked around the room, telling herself not to be stupid. Everyone does it. There's no need to start behaving like a Victorian bride. She tried to imagine herself as the sort of woman she read about in *Cosmopolitan* magazine – assured, knowledgeable, demanding.

"There isn't anywhere to put our stuff," Paul said. There was a stack of bags and belongings in one corner, with several of Paul's T-shirts draped over the top. Crumpled sheets and a plaid blanket were spread over the mattress, and the carpet was threadbare, frayed at the edges. Abigail was dismayed by the dinginess of it all. She hadn't expected frilly cushions or deep-pile carpets or *Ideal Home* colour co-ordination, but all the same . . .

"At least there are curtains," she said, moving to the window.

Paul came to stand beside her and rested a hand on her shoulder, his fingers stroking her neck. It will be all right, she told herself. Paul's here, and what else could I want?

"You can just about see the sea," he said, "if you crane your neck to the left. Sea view, hot and cold running water – well, hot when we remember to put the boiler on – all mod cons. I think you've seen all the cons now. They'll do, even if they aren't very mod. Let's go down and get a drink."

As they went downstairs the front door opened, and Jess and Bill came in carrying paper-wrapped packages and bringing a steamy fishy smell with them.

"Hi, Abby." Bill looked at her in his owlish way. "Glad you could make it."

"We didn't get you any fish and chips," Jess said. "We could have, if we'd known you'd be here."

Abigail realized that she was very hungry, and it occurred to her that she wasn't going to be presented with meals at regular times, not any more. She could have devoured one of Mum's shepherd's pies. She wondered what arrangements there were for shopping and cooking, or even whether there *were* any arrangements – it looked rather as if people fended for themselves. She looked wistfully at the sagging parcel in Jess's hands.

"No sweat," Paul said. "We'll go out and get a pizza or something."

Jess went into the kitchen and started complaining loudly about the washing-up left in the sink and the lack of clean plates, and Paul grinned at Abigail and said, "Time to do a vanishing act."

They went to Pizzaland in the town centre and shared a big pizza and salad, with ice cream and coffee afterwards. Mentally totting up how much it would all cost, Abigail began to worry about money. She had brought all she had, but the train fares had been more than five pounds, and this was an expensive way to eat. Perhaps she ought to start looking for a job straight away.

"You don't think your parents will get the police looking for you, do you?" Paul said, as they sat over their coffee. "You're not eighteen yet."

"I suppose it *is* quite likely. But they won't have any idea where I am. I've been talking about working in London for the summer and they probably think I've gone there – that's where most people go, isn't it? I haven't told anyone at all. The only way they could find out is by getting in touch with your parents. They don't know your surname but I suppose they could get that from college."

"That's all right, then." Paul sipped his coffee and put more sugar in it. "My parents don't know where I am, either."

She stared at him. "*Yours* don't? Why didn't you tell them?"

"Just didn't bother. They think I'm bumming round Europe. They know I'll turn up again when it suits me. They won't start panicking."

Abigail wondered how true this was. Parents, in her experience, weren't like that.

"I'll be eighteen at the beginning of September. Then we needn't worry. I can do what I like," she said. She flattened the bill between her fingers and remembered the money problem. "Where can I look for a job?"

"The local paper comes out on Thursdays. Or look in shop windows and restaurants. I think I've got a job lined up, for myself," Paul said. "In the pub by the harbour. I'm going round tomorrow lunchtime. If they take me on I'll start straight away."

"What are we paying for rent?"

"Five pounds a week," Paul said.

"Oh, that's not too bad. Two-fifty each."

"No, I mean five pounds each. Plus our share of the bills. But that shouldn't be much, this time of year."

"OK." Abigail realized that she had no idea at all how much things cost, or ought to cost. "I'll definitely look for a job, then."

Paul smiled. "But tonight we're on holiday. Let's pay our bill and go. It's still light enough for a walk along the beach."

This was as Abigail had imagined it, domestic

worries vanishing as they went out into the dusk and walked along to the promenade. It was still quite warm, although a breeze chilled the air as they reached the seafront. Coloured lights strung between the lamp-posts gave a festive air. The tide was high, covering the sand completely, leaving only pebble banks uncovered below the protective wall. Abigail and Paul ran down to the steps and along the shingle, their shoes crunching and slithering on the rounded stones. Paul stooped to choose flattened pebbles and flicked them into the water so that they bounced over the surface. Abigail watched him, soothed by the lull of the waves and the gentle hiss and roll as they fell back, dragging at the pebbles. There was still a sunset glow to the west, rose-pink fading into smudges of cloud. Along the beach, below the stacks of deckchairs, someone was throwing a stick for a dog, which plunged and yapped after it into the sea.

"There's a little cove on the other side of those rocks," Paul said, "where not many people go."

He started to walk along, his back to the sunset. Abigail hoped he wasn't going to suggest rock-climbing, not in the near-dark. When he reached a platform of rock jutting into the sea he vaulted up easily and then held out his hand for her, and she saw that it was only a scramble to reach the little bay on the other side. It was a private, enclosed place, sheltered by arms of rock. Pale sand stretched into the mouth of a cave. The rock face was smooth and black in the half-light. Abigail could smell the salty dampness of seaweed; the tide must have turned.

"There's always a bit of sand left here, even at high tide," Paul said.

Abigail's shoes sank into the damp sand. She moved closer to the water and sat on a ledge of rock, looking out to sea. "It's so peaceful. You can't see the lights of the town any more. We could be miles from anywhere."

It was real untamed sea here, not like the town beach where it was concreted and groyned and fenced. Here, the sea defined its own boundaries – cave, promontory, overhang.

Paul knelt in front of Abigail and twined his arms round her neck. "This is perfect," he said softly.

Her arms went round his body and their lips met, tasting of salt. Abigail shivered with excitement. Tonight there would be no dash home, no hasty last kisses, no creeping indoors to evade angry parents. They would stay together. They would go back to the house and up to their room, and Jess and Bill would know what they were going to do. And in the morning she would have to face them again and they would know.

Perhaps it didn't have to be like that. It was perfect here, Paul had just said so: the cool salty air, the tingling half-darkness, the dying glow of the sunset, the turning tide. She could make it happen, now. She tightened her arms around Paul and he pulled her down off the rock, to the damp sand. She slid a hand inside his T-shirt and over the smooth skin of his back. His body was lithe and eager, full of taut energy, like an instrument she could learn to play. She could feel his breathing against her neck and his hands were inside her jumper, cool and then warm, smoothing, searching, unfastening. It was going to be easy, as natural as the rise and fall of the waves . . .

Then he pulled away. She wondered whether she had done something wrong. She couldn't see his expression, only the gleam of his teeth as he turned away from her.

"Let's go back," he said. His voice sounded different, husky.

"Can't we – you know, here—"

He made a gesture of frustration. "The rubbers – I haven't got them with me. I should have put them in my pocket." He stood up and pulled her to her feet, brushing the damp sand off her jeans and jumper. "Daft, isn't it?"

She hadn't even thought of that, in her eagerness. "I'm sorry."

He laughed, turning it into a joke. "Doesn't

matter. I should have known you wouldn't be able to keep your hands off me. Come on, let's go back."

Tuesday 16 July

I suppose I should feel different, but I don't, not really. I thought it would be like reaching the other side of a Great Divide. Before and After. But it isn't.

To be perfectly honest, the first thing I felt was *Is that it?* I mean, I've read *Cosmopolitan* and the rude bits in *Lady Chatterley's Lover*. It hardly seemed to be the same thing at all. It wasn't what I imagined, when we were down by the rocks. But at least Paul didn't seem to think I was hopeless, and it's over now, the first time. I expect you get better at it, like learning to drive. I felt as if everyone would be able to tell when I went downstairs this morning, and they'd laugh at me. But when I said so to Paul, he said don't be so silly and why should they? It doesn't matter to them in the least. And of course he was right. They were too busy burning toast to take any notice.

I wrote *everyone* just now but actually I haven't met everyone yet. Just a glimpse of the guy called Beano, going out. He's got a black beard and so much hair that you can hardly see his face. I haven't heard Gillian at all. Paul says she keeps herself to herself. It's not much like I expected, really. I thought it would be more like a party here. But I won't say any more, in case someone reads this.

There was a knock at the bedroom door and Abigail hastily shoved her diary and pen under the mattress. "Come in."

It was Jess. She glanced down at the dishevelled bed and Abigail felt herself blushing. She hated blushing, because people at school had always joked about it clashing with her hair. Jess had an expressionless way of looking at people which made Abigail feel uneasy. She couldn't imagine becoming friendly with Jess.

"I thought you were in," Jess said. "Where's Paul?"

"Gone to the pub about a job."

Jess nodded, and said, "Look, could you go and get some shopping, if you've nothing else to do? We used up the last of the bread this morning, and we're out of things like bog roll. I've just nipped back to get something but I need to get back to the gallery."

Abigail agreed, and got up.

"Come on down then and I'll write out a list."

They went into the kitchen, where the sink was still piled with greasy plates, and Jess started to make a list. She didn't say anything about money and Abigail wondered whether she would have enough to pay for it all. She watched Jess adding more and more items. Her writing was very stylized, with long curved hooks. The combination of mundane household items with such consciously artistic handwriting seemed incongruous.

"Have you got another key?" Abigail asked. "Paul and I have only got one between us."

"Get one cut while you're in town," Jess said, as if it were a silly question. "See you later, then."

She handed over the list. When she had gone, Abigail fetched the free local paper and looked at the jobs pages to ring round any vacancies that looked suitable. Most of them weren't. There were several advertisements for bar staff, but she was too young to work in a pub. There was one for a children's nanny, but that would mean long unsociable hours, and she didn't think she could cope with young children. All that was left was the shoe-shop. She decided to go there first.

She walked the long way round, just for the pleasure of strolling along by the seafront. The sky was blue, streaked with high cirrus cloud, and a light breeze stirred her hair. Gulls screamed and wheeled, their cries lifting Abigail's spirits. She felt like running, like a little child, dashing down to the sea and plunging into it, in the lovely exhilaration of her new freedom. Along the sea wall, by the harbour, was Drake's Drum, the pub where Paul had gone. As he hadn't come back, he must be in there working. Even though she wasn't with him Abigail felt that there was an invisible link between them. They belonged to each other now, not in any old-fashioned possessive way, but because they loved each other. She wondered whether to burst in and surprise him, thought better of it and turned back reluctantly to the High Street and her errands.

"Sorry, the vacancy's been filled," the shoe-shop manager told her.

Abigail hadn't really wanted it anyway. Nine to five-thirty, with Saturdays, was too long. She wanted casual work, a few hours a day, just enough to pay for her keep. She got the key cut and went to the supermarket, where she wandered around with a trolley trying to find all the things Jess had specified. The list said "meat", which sounded straightforward enough, but the meat counter presented an overwhelming choice. There were legs of lamb and joints of beef and whole chickens, but Abigail couldn't imagine anything as ambitious as a roast dinner emerging from the grimy kitchen of 32 Princeton Terrace. She looked at a cut of beef called silverside, but that was alarmingly expensive at sixty-nine pence per pound.

Stewing steak was much cheaper, so she chose some of that, and added a packet of bacon.

"Three pounds sixty-seven and a half," the checkout girl said in bored voice. Abigail counted it out. The contents of her purse were vanishing rapidly. She would *have* to find some work, quickly, or not eat. She enquired about vacancies for checkout assistants, but the manager said the store was fully staffed.

No one appeared to be in when she got back to the house. The kitchen still smelled of the morning's burnt toast. The cooker was coated with grease and burnt-on stains, and there was a bag full of smelly rubbish by the sink. She unpacked the shopping and decided to tidy up. She took a decaying half-cucumber and a piece of mouldy cheese-rind out of the fridge and threw them in the rubbish bag, then embarked on the washing-up, which meant boiling a kettle first as the boiler wasn't on – she had had to wash in cold water when she got up. When she had done that, and cleaned the sink, she took the rubbish bags out to the bins. She was feeling virtuous and wondering whether to tackle the cooker when Bill and Jess came in.

"Did you get everything?" Jess said. "Let's get the kettle on. I'm dying of thirst."

She made no mention of the clean shiny sink or the lack of clutter, but when she looked in the fridge she took out the stewing steak and said, "What did you get this for? This is no good."

"It was cheap," Abigail defended herself. "You didn't say what sort of meat you wanted."

"I meant things you can cook under the grill, like sausages or chops," Jess said. "I thought that was obvious. What are we supposed to do with this?"

"Stew it, I suppose."

"If you fancy messing about with onions and stock, you're welcome," Jess said.

"A casserole. That'd be nice," Bill said, coming to Abigail's aid. "I'm fed up with sausages and takeaways."

"I'll make one then." Abigail was annoyed with Jess. How had Jess expected her to know? "If you show me how to light the oven."

"You'll have to go out shopping again for the other stuff you'll need," Jess said. "We don't usually go in for home cooking. I'd no idea you were going to come here and start domesticating us."

"I suppose there isn't a recipe book anywhere?" Abigail ignored the taunt.

"*Recipe* book? You're joking," Jess said. "Do you want some tea? We ought to get some new mugs. Most of these are chipped."

"No thanks. I'm going out for onions and stuff. And could you give me some money? The shopping was three sixty-something and I'm practically broke."

Jess searched lengthily in her dungarees pockets and produced fifty pence, and then Bill handed over a crumpled pound note. Abigail went out again, wishing Paul would come back. Presumably, he'd have to work evenings as well, so she would have to get used to spending time on her own. Or else hang around the pub, which she wouldn't be able to afford. She didn't fancy spending too much time at the house when Jess was there. Jess could at least have noticed the clearing-up she had done, instead of mocking her for being domesticated. That's a laugh, she thought: me, domesticated! What would Mum say if she heard that? She used to joke that I'd die of starvation if I had to fend for myself. But Mum would have more than one shock, if she could see the set-up here . . .

She didn't want to think about Mum and home. First she was going to the library, to borrow a cookery book and find out what you did with stewing steak. It felt odd filling in a card, using her new address for the first time. She found a book and went with it to the supermarket and got what she needed: cooking oil, stock cubes, carrots, black pepper. If she was going to do this, she was going to do it properly.

Thursday 18 July

I've got a job. I start tomorrow.

Met Gillian today. I think I like her. She's nothing like the others.

"Twelve till six, with a half-hour break."

"That'll be fine," Abigail said.

"Only till the end of the season, mind." Having offered Abigail the job, the proprietress now appeared suspicious, as if fearing she'd made a mistake. Her name was Mrs Trelawney and she was very neatly turned out: hair permed into stiff grey waves, pearl earrings, a pink blouse with a lace collar. She matched the decor of the Harbour Lights Café. Each table had a pink cloth with a lace one over the top, and dotted around the pink walls were cute little pictures of children in frilly knickers, waving buckets and spades and building sandcastles. Paul or Jess would have made retching noises. Abigail smiled politely and said, "Yes, that'll be fine, thank you." Her demure grammar-school-girl manner, long discarded but resurrected for the occasion, had done the trick.

"You'll need to wear a black skirt, black shoes – clean, of course – and a nice blouse," Mrs Trelawney said, looking doubtfully at Abigail's patched jeans and striped T-shirt. "I'll provide you with a clean apron every day. Hair tied back in a ponytail or plait, please, dear. We can't have loose hairs getting into the food."

She was going to be fussy, obviously. The kitchen at the back, where she baked scones and cakes, was pristine, every surface gleaming, nothing left lying around. If Mrs Trelawney could see the kitchen at Princeton Terrace she'd have apoplexy. But the job was a bit of luck – five afternoons a week, and all the mornings off. That would fit in quite well with Paul's hours, and Drake's Drum was handy, on the opposite side of the harbour. The money problems would be taken care of.

"I'll need a reference," Mrs Trelawney added. "The baker's shop you mentioned would do."

Abigail thought quickly. She couldn't give the baker's at home, in case her mother went into the shop and someone mentioned it. "Er – they've closed down," she said.

"Is there someone who can give you a personal reference? I usually do take them up, just in case," Mrs Trelawney persisted. "You never know in a place like this. People come and go so quickly."

"I could give you the name of my school," Abigail said in desperation.

"Yes, all right, dear. Write it down here, next to your address. You're not on the phone at home, you say? That's a pity. I'll see you tomorrow, then, twelve o'clock sharp."

Mrs Trelawney nodded briskly and Abigail went out into the sunshine. Luckily, she did have a black skirt – wraparound cheesecloth and ankle-length, certainly not what Mrs Trelawney had in mind, but black nevertheless – and one white blouse which would do, of embroidered Indian cotton. She would have to wash it out every night. Washing clothes was another of the practicalities she hadn't yet got to grips with. Various shapeless garments had been hanging on a washing line in the back garden ever since she had arrived, but she thought it might be easier to take her washing and Paul's to the launderette. There was so much to do, just looking after yourself, that she wondered how on earth people managed it. But she was learning to adapt to Paul's no-worries attitude. Nothing mattered all that much.

She let herself indoors, wishing there was someone at home to share her triumph. Music floated down from the top floor, Pink Floyd, which meant that Beano was in, but he wouldn't be interested. Abigail had still seen little of the elusive Gillian beyond brief meetings in the doorway of the loo or bathroom. She was striking in appearance: tall, with short dark hair shaped to her head, and slightly olive skin. She seemed friendly enough, but always went straight up to her room and stayed there. She had been invited to have some of

Abigail's casserole on Monday night but had said that she didn't eat meat. Abigail wondered what she did up there in her room all day.

In the bedroom, Abigail sorted out her clothes for tomorrow. They were badly crumpled and she wondered whether there was such a thing as an iron in the house. She doubted it. Bill and Jess's clothes, and Paul's for that matter, always looked as if they'd been picked up from a heap on the floor.

Deciding to try Gillian, she climbed the narrow stairs to the top floor. The Pink Floyd was coming from the front room, above hers and Paul's. She knocked on the other door, which was adorned with a macramé hanging in the shape of an exotic bird, strung with beads.

"Come in," Gillian's voice said.

Abigail did so. Gillian was sitting by the window, painting. She wore a turquoise Indian scarf tied round her head so that none of her hair showed. Abigail looked round the room in surprise; it looked so much more inhabited than anywhere else in the house. There were woven rugs on the floor, hangings and paintings on the walls, and a patchwork quilt thrown over the single bed, a proper bed. Even a couple of cane chairs, with cushions. The room smelled of oil paint and spicy perfume.

"Come in," Gillian said again, as Abigail hesitated in the doorway. "I was just going to have some coffee – would you like some?"

She stood up from her easel. Abigail would have liked to see what she was painting, but it faced away from her. There were other canvases too, stacked against the wall.

"Thanks," Abigail said. Gillian took mugs from a cupboard, and a packet of coffee. She crouched on the floor making proper coffee, not instant, with a filter arrangement which she filled with water from a jug. She even had a little two-ring heater and a bowl for washing-up, which explained why she appeared so rarely in the kitchen. Abigail had been wondering whether she ever ate at all. She sat down on the bed and watched fascinated as Gillian got everything ready. It all seemed so orderly, especially seen fresh from the muddle the rest of the household lived in.

"I don't have milk," Gillian said over her shoulder. "I can get some from downstairs if you take it."

"No, black's all right, thanks."

The room began to fill with the wonderful smell of roast coffee. Gillian stood up and looked at Abigail with speculative interest. She wore a long batik skirt and a cobalt-blue fisherman's smock with paint splodges on it. The Indian scarf round her head made her look exotic; she had a delicate, high-cheekboned face, with dark eyes.

"So," she said, "what are you doing here?"

"I came to see if you had an iron," Abigail explained.

"No, I mean here in Devon."

"I'm living with Paul," Abigail said, rather defiantly, as if Gillian were the sort of person to disapprove. "We're going to spend the summer drawing and painting." Nothing at all had been done so far in that direction, she realized; neither of them had so much as taken out a pencil or sketchpad.

"What do you draw and paint?" Gillian asked.

"Well, nothing really yet," Abigail admitted. "I don't know if I'm any good."

"There's only one way to find out," Gillian said.

"What about you?" Abigail asked. "Have you been here a long time? It looks so comfortable here."

"Since last winter. There were some students from Exeter here then, friends of Beano's. He's been here about a year."

Abigail glanced towards the stacked canvases. "Are you an art student?"

"No. Only in my own way. I just paint."

"You make a living by painting, then?"

Gillian smiled. "That's not very easy, but I just about manage. I do a bit of commercial work, illustrating gardening books. But I'd like to drop that and concentrate on my own stuff."

Abigail was surprised. Paul always spoke of commercial work as if it were tainted, not something any serious artist would consider. But Gillian clearly *was* serious about herself. She made Abigail think of Patrick Leary, her grandfather: Gillian apparently had the same sort of dedication. She didn't seem to need a social life, or boyfriends, according to what the others said.

"Do you sell any of your pictures?" Abigail asked.

"One of the galleries in Exeter likes them and I've sold a few things there. Before I came here I worked for three years, all sorts of odd jobs, and saved as much money as I could. Now I've earned the chance to see if I can make a go of it. I can live pretty cheaply here."

Abigail wished she could look at the paintings, but didn't like to ask. Gillian poured out the black coffee and handed her a mug.

"Do you ever see anything of Bill's uncle, the one who owns the house?" Abigail asked.

"I've met him a couple of times. In the winter he had to come down and sort out the plumbing. He bought the house to do it up and sell it. He doesn't plan to live here. He's got his own house at Totnes."

"So he'll want us all to move out soon?" Abigail was alarmed; the house was starting to feel like – well, not like home, but like a base, a kind of territory, hers and Paul's.

"I shouldn't worry." Gillian passed over a tin of biscuits. "He's the sort of person who starts things and never finishes them. He's probably realized that he can make money out of the house just as it is, by letting it to students. I doubt if he'll bother."

"Perhaps you'll be able to sell some of your work when Jess and Bill open their gallery?" Abigail suggested.

Gillian looked at her with an odd half-smile. "Perhaps. But I don't know how long that will be. Have you seen it?"

"Not yet."

Abigail remembered her ironing, and told Gillian about her job at the Harbour Lights Café. Gillian fetched the iron and ironing-board out of her wardrobe. When she had finished her coffee Abigail got up to go, and Gillian said, "Come up again, if you feel like it. I don't mind being interrupted. And do get on with the drawing, if you're serious about it."

Friday 19 July

Raining. We stayed in bed late and probably wouldn't have got up at all if we didn't have to go to work.

I don't mind any more what the others think, now that I'm used to it. No one takes any notice of anyone else, anyway. I expect Jess envies me. Bill's quite nice but you couldn't call him *attractive*, not like Paul.

I started a drawing near the harbour yesterday afternoon when I came down from Gillian's, and did some more when I left the café. I showed it to Paul last night and he said it was a bit conventional but not bad. He said I'm good for him because he's too lazy to work if he's left on his own. He said I've got to bully him and make him get his paints out next time he has a day off. I expect he needs a break after doing all that work for the exhibition.

Waking to the sound of rain lashing the window, Abigail stretched up a hand to pull back the bit of curtain she could reach. Paul was asleep, his face crumpled into the pillow. She loved looking at him while he was sleeping. He had long eyelashes, and lids delicately veined with blue. As she watched him, his eyes opened and he stirred. He looked at her and smiled slowly, and then stretched out with lazy enjoyment, like a cat.

"Come here." He reached out and pulled her back into the warm cave of bedclothes.

She snuggled into his embrace. "It's a quarter to nine, and pouring with rain," she told him.

"Why do you sound so pleased about it?"

"Because I'm thinking of everyone going to work, getting on trains and buses and going off to their boring old offices and factories and shops. While we can stay here. I'm going to put the boiler on and have a long soak in the bath."

"You're going to work too."

"Yes, but not until twelve and I'll finish at six o'clock, and it'll stop raining by then and be lovely and sunny. And you're not working tonight. You can come and meet me, and we can get fish and chips and eat them by the harbour, and then walk along the estuary."

"Mmm. And then come back and have a drink in the pub garden."

"And go for a boat trip! I haven't had a boat trip yet! There's a little cruiser that goes from the harbour every evening. We can go just as it's starting to get dark, and see the sunset and the town lighting up. Let's be tourists, just for this evening."

"Mmm. And then come back to bed." Paul's eyes had closed again and his arms were wound tightly round her, but after a few moments he wriggled free and pushed the bedclothes back and stood up, rubbing his eyes.

She watched him. "Are you getting up?"

"Just going for a pee."

He was opening the bedroom door. Abigail sat up and pulled the sheet round her shoulders. "You shouldn't walk about with nothing on!" she told him. "Someone might see you."

"I don't suppose they'll see anything they haven't seen before. Anyway, Jess and Bill have gone out. I heard them."

"But Gillian. She might come down."

"Lucky her, then. Make her day."

"Oh, you—" She slumped back on the mattress. "You're so conceited!"

He grinned and came to her and crouched by the bed, twisting his fingers into her tangle of hair. "I know. And you're such a prude, aren't you? What would Mummy and Daddy say if they could see you now?"

"Not that much of a prude," she pointed out, "or I wouldn't be here at all."

"All right then, Miss Only Slightly Prudish. I'll go and make some tea. Don't get up, I'm coming back to bed."

Mrs Trelawney wasn't too impressed by the outfit.

"It's not quite the standard of smartness I expect from my waitresses. It looks a bit hippyish."

"I'm sorry, but I haven't got anything else."

"And those *shoes*. Plimsolls! I can't have you wearing plimsolls here. It's not that sort of establishment."

"Well, I haven't got any smart black shoes.

And I can't afford to buy any."

Mrs Trelawney sighed. "Well, I suppose the skirt's long enough to hide them. They'll have to do for now. But I'm not happy about it."

Abigail had to stifle a giggle at the vision of outraged customers stomping out, complaining, "I can't possibly drink tea served by a girl in *plimsolls . . .*'

She didn't hide it very well. Mrs Trelawney said sharply, "I'm not amused, dear. I run things properly here. I've got standards. Perhaps we'd better regard this afternoon as a trial period."

Abigail straightened her face. Better be extra polite to the customers. She didn't want to lose her job on the day she started it.

She spent the next few hours trotting obediently to and fro, smiling nicely at everyone. The café was busy all afternoon, with a quick turnover since it served nothing more substantial than scones and cakes. Abigail managed not to be impatient with dithering customers or spill tea over them, and some of them even left tips. She scrupulously took all of these back to the kitchen, where Mrs Trelawney told her to put them in a plate.

"Don't forget the tips. They're yours," Mrs Trelawney told her at six o'clock.

Abigail was surprised. There must be more than fifty pence in that plate. This was an unexpected bonus.

"I'll see you tomorrow, then, dear. You'll do," Mrs Trelawney said, flipping over the OPEN sign on the door so that it read CLOSED. "You can put the tips towards a decent pair of shoes. Or perhaps your parents might buy you some?"

"I don't live with my parents," Abigail said. "I'm staying with relations."

Mrs Trelawney seemed to have an inbuilt lie-detector, for she gave Abigail a doubtful look. But she said nothing, and Abigail left feeling pleased with her afternoon's work and the extra money. She wondered whether to go over to the pub and see Paul, but it was such a gorgeous evening, fresh-washed and clear after the morning's rain, that she decided to sit on the shingle bank beyond the harbour and continue with her drawing. It was a simple sketch of an overturned rowing-boat pulled up high on the shingle, looking as if it belonged to nobody, with dried-out boards and cracked paint. She was attracted by the curve of the planking and the way the boat nestled into the stones, its colours fading as if in camouflage. She took out her sketchpad and pencils from her bag and threw down an old jumper to sit on. She sat for a few minutes enjoying the sun on her face and the smell of fish and salt and dried seaweed. Then she picked up her pencil, and was soon absorbed in the drawing.

Part Three

*I*t seemed for a while as if it would always be like that: summer would go on for ever, the sun would shine, everything would work out just as we wanted it. We had each other, and that was all that mattered.

It's all stayed with me so vividly. Even now, I've only got to hear the cry of gulls or see a fishing harbour, or smell that fishy seaweed smell or taste the salt wind on my lips, and I'm back there. That summer.

* * * * *

Sunday 18 August

We had a row today. Our first real row, a horrible one. And it was all my fault. I provoked him into it. I can't stand it. I don't know what to do.

I don't think Paul loves me as much as I love him.

The tourist season was in full flow. The café was busy all day: families with small children trailing sand across the pink carpet; pensioners on coach outings; honeymoon couples holding hands across the table. Tanned, beautiful people from the yachts that stayed briefly in the harbour and then headed off for France or the Isles of Scilly.

The Harbour Lights Café was too *genteel* to attract the Hell's Angels or the penniless hitch-hikers who contributed to the shifting population of Chilcombe Sands. There were trendier, more casual places to attract them, like the Souk on the High Street, whose dark, bazaar-style interior emitted sitar music by day and loud rock by night. Abigail sometimes wished she worked there instead, but was too comfortable in her niche to bother making a change. Paul teased her about it. "You like it there really. You and Mother T. suit each other, don't you?" Abigail had even gone so far as to comply with Mrs Trelawney's footwear requirements by buying some cheap canvas pumps. They weren't a lot smarter than the plimsolls, but Mrs Trelawney seemed pleased.

Abigail was conscientiously doing some drawing every day now, before or after work, sometimes both. It was like physical exercise, she decided; regular practice freed you from constriction and stiffness, keeping the drawing muscles flexed. She always drew in soft pencil. Paul had started to paint spasmodically; sometimes they would work together, though she found him a twitchy and irritating companion in this respect. He would paint feverishly for two hours and then throw down his brush in frustration and do no more for a week. He would never discuss his work. Abigail thought he had a true artistic temperament; she was a mere plodder, making the most of what little talent she had.

Her drawings were improving, though uninspired. She wanted lessons, really, but when she asked Paul for advice he was dismissive, saying that representational drawing wasn't his thing. Gillian was more help. "You want to go for a bolder, cleaner line," she told Abigail. "Don't fuss and dither. See what you want to do and do it without hesitation. It's no good fidgeting about and thinking it'll somehow materialize. It won't. Every time you put your pencil to paper it's got to mean something." Abigail tried to follow her advice. She liked to draw small manageable things: a lobster pot, a cottage door, a moored dinghy.

Sometimes people, although she found that more difficult.

Sunday evening: her day off tomorrow, and Paul's. She followed Mrs Trelawney out of the café, deciding to go over to the pub to meet him. On Friday and Saturday nights, Drake's Drum was crowded with locals as well as tourists and there was often live music, but Sunday evenings were quieter, especially at this early hour. They could have a drink together and plan their free day.

The interior of the pub had a nautical flavour. Fishing nets, glass weights and compasses were hung around the walls, with the occasional stuffed fish in a glass case. A noisy sailing group occupied a corner table and Stuart, one of the bar staff, was drying glasses at the bar, but there was no sign of Paul.

"Gone out the back, I think." Stuart jerked a thumb towards the door which led to the rear garden.

Abigail went through. There were wooden tables outside on a rise overlooking the harbour and bay. The garden was empty apart from Paul and a blonde girl, talking. The girl sat at one of the tables and Paul stood with one foot on the wooden bench, leaning forward attentively. He said something Abigail couldn't hear and the girl laughed, throwing her head back and shaking out her long hair. Abigail stopped dead for a moment before crossing the grass towards them, feeling like an intruder. She told herself not to be stupid: Paul was talking to a girl, but what of it? He must meet dozens of girls every day at the bar.

They both turned to look at her. Paul moved slightly farther away and said easily, "Oh, hi, Abby. You didn't say you were coming over. Claudia, this is Abby."

"Pleased to meet you," Claudia said in a German accent, smiling at Abigail. She had clear tanned skin and very blue eyes, and wore a yellow T-shirt with lacing at the front.

"Hello," Abigail said. She wished Paul had said, "This is my girlfriend Abby," or "This is Abby, who I live with," or had put his arm round her, so that Claudia would recognize their relationship. *Keep off, he's mine, he belongs to me*, was what she wanted to say. It was the kind of attitude she would have despised in anyone else. Relationships did not mean possession; she and Paul were in agreement about that. In theory, at any rate. Just seeing him bending towards Claudia like that had turned something over inside her.

"I start work here next week," Claudia said. "Paul is helping me to learn what I will be doing."

"Here, in the pub?" Abigail looked sharply at Paul. "You didn't tell me there was a job going!"

"You too would have wanted it?" Claudia said. "Then perhaps I am lucky you didn't know."

"Abby's already got a job," Paul said. "You know you couldn't have applied, not till you're eighteen," he said to Abigail.

"But that's only two weeks away!"

"The landlord can't wait two weeks. Not in the middle of August."

Claudia was looking at them doubtfully, from one to the other. "I am sorry. I do not mean to make trouble."

"It's all right. You've got the job. Don't worry about it," Paul said.

"Well, I must go. I see you on Tuesday, Paul. Goodbye, Abby. I see you again perhaps." Claudia bent down for her shoulder bag which was lying on the ground, and her long blonde hair slithered over her face. She flicked it back as she stood up, smiled at them both charmingly and went into the pub. Paul stooped to pick up a discarded crisp packet, not looking at Abigail. She thought of him and Claudia together in the cramped space behind the bar, sidling round each other, laughing, sharing jokes.

"You didn't even *mention* the job!" she accused.

"What was the point? I forgot, anyhow." He walked towards the rubbish bin with his characteristic slack-hipped saunter. Usually

Abigail loved the arrogant, cocky way he walked, but now she felt like hitting him.

"You *forgot* – how could you, when you knew I wanted something better than dreary old Mrs T.?"

"Oh, come on – you like it there with the old dear. You've never bothered to try for anything else. You can't expect the pub to go short-staffed for a fortnight just because you fancy working here. There was no shortage of applicants." He turned to face her, smiling derisively. "What did you want me to say, then – there's a job going, but I'm sorry, you can't have it?"

"Yes. That is what I wanted you to say."

Paul shrugged, as if to indicate that the workings of her mind were unfathomable to the normal reasonable male.

"Anyway, I don't think it would be such a good idea," he said. "We shouldn't work together. It'd be stifling, being together all the time."

"It'd cramp your style, you mean," she flared. "You might not be able to chat up other girls so easily if I was watching."

He sighed exaggeratedly. "For Christ's sake, Abby, don't start that whole jealousy bit."

"I'm not jealous," she lied.

"Oh yeah? Isn't that why you came over just now, to check up on me?"

"Of course not! I just wanted to see you!" Her voice wavered as her vision of their lovely leisurely day off together cracked into jagged pieces. "I suppose you can't understand that?"

"Then don't be so bloody stupid. Just because I was talking to someone else."

"It's not just that," she cried, close to tears. "You don't understand! You think I'm *stifling* you! You were the one who wanted me to come away with you – now you're bored with me, I suppose!"

"I never said that. Don't get hysterical, for Christ's sake," Paul said wearily. "But I don't belong to you. I'm not into all that clingy business."

"Neither am I!"

The clink of glass sounded in the doorway and Stuart stepped outside with a crate of empty bottles. Abigail wondered whether he had overheard them arguing. She lowered her voice and said, "I'm not being possessive. I'm disappointed because there was a job and somebody else got it."

"Only because you don't like the idea of me working with Claudia."

"Oh, of course! You're conceited enough to think no girl can resist you!"

He glared at her. "If I'm only imagining it, then what are you worrying about?"

"Yes, why should I care? What does it matter to me?" She knew that she was sounding more and more ridiculous, contradicting herself, but she couldn't stop.

"Don't try to tie me down," Paul said, in a voice quiet with controlled anger. "It won't work. I do my own thing."

"What are you saying?" she retorted. "That you want to go out with other girls? Go on, then, and see if I care!"

Paul looked at her for a moment without speaking, his mouth set in a tight line. He could have been a stranger; Abigail felt as if she didn't know him at all. He laughed, a short unamused laugh, and said, "You'd better go. I've got work to do. And for God's sake snap out of it."

"Don't worry, I'm going. You make me feel sick."

Suddenly she had to get away from him. She stumbled across to the side gate, tears blurring her vision. The gate catch was stiff and she took a few moments to open it, more than she needed, giving him plenty of time to run to her and say, "Abby, I'm sorry. I didn't mean it. I love you."

But he didn't.

The evening dragged past reluctantly, as if time itself were trying to prolong her misery. Abigail had no idea what to do with herself, where to go. It would be hopeless trying to draw and she could not face going back to the house with her eyes red from crying. In the end she just walked about, and sat for ages in one of the rain shelters, brooding. Paul would be pulling pints in the bar, chatting to customers, eyeing the prettiest girls, probably not sparing her a thought. He was bored with her; she wasn't exciting enough for him. He felt stifled by her, she was tedious, a drag, a handicap.

I love him too much, she thought.

Everyone who passed by looked happy and purposeful: couples and groups and families, heading for their holiday flats or their evening out. Even Mum and Dad and Rachel would be on holiday now, in the north of Scotland. She imagined them enjoying themselves without her, not even thinking about her. She wondered if they spoke about her in the past tense, like someone who had died. If Paul didn't want her she might as well die.

A breeze was rising and eventually it was too cold to hang about any longer. She went home and got ready for bed. She looked at her watch; Paul wouldn't be home for another hour and a half, at least. When he was in the room with her, it was their own place, their private sanctuary. But now she noticed the damp patches on the wall and the frayed, dirty carpet, and the curtains that didn't quite meet in the middle. The sheets needed washing, too. It was such a drag, humping great bundles off to the launderette. She had meant to do something about the room, especially since seeing Gillian's, to make it more like a proper home, but she hadn't done anything more ambitious than sticking a small print of Monet's *Les Coquelicots* on the wall.

Without Paul, it was a dismal squat.

It frightened her to realize how much she depended on him. Without him, she would lose her reason for being here; she would lose her home, and such friends as she had. More than that, she would lose her self-esteem; she felt as if he were part of her, giving her the courage to persevere with this makeshift new life, giving it a meaning.

When he came back it would be all right. She would stay awake and wait for him to come to bed, and she would apologize for being petty and unreasonable and he would forgive her.

But it didn't work out like that. In spite of herself she drifted off to sleep, and only woke up when she realized that he was getting into bed, yanking at the covers and bringing with him the smoky pub smell which she usually complained about. He didn't speak to her, or touch her. She rolled towards him and put an arm round him, but he shrugged her off irritably and moved to the farthest edge of the mattress, huddling himself tightly into the sheet. He was soon asleep, not hearing her crying, or taking any notice if he did.

Monday 19 August

It's all right now. As if it never happened. I was so stupid.

Abigail slept fitfully and woke in the early morning tired and drained, her eyes aching. Paul was still asleep, turned away from her in a forbidding hump. She got up and went to the bathroom and looked at herself in the cracked mirror. Her eyelids were puffy but otherwise she didn't look as ghastly as she felt.

The house was quiet; no one else seemed to be up. Sunlight streamed through the dirty windows, illuminating the grimy cracked lino of the bathroom floor. She had intended to make tea for Paul and try to salvage something of their free day, but now she changed her mind. She wanted to be outside, by the sea, away from Paul, away from everyone. She wanted him to wake up and find her gone. She couldn't bear him to look at her in that cold hard way that made him seem like a stranger.

Back in their room she dressed as quietly as she could. Searching for a clean T-shirt in the heap of clothes, she knocked against a box of Paul's painting stuff, sending tubes of acrylic rattling to the floor. She scooped them up quickly and pushed them back in place. There was a muffled groan from the bed and Paul rolled over, opening his eyes and then screwing them up tightly.

"What time is it?" he asked, as if nothing had happened.

"Half-past seven."

He propped himself up to look at her, raising a hand to rub bleary eyes. "What are you doing?"

"Just getting dressed," she said defensively.

"What for?"

She hesitated, trying to gauge his mood. He was nearly awake now and his face was serious, a little concerned, but not angry any more; he looked as if he might smile and become his normal self again. She wavered, gave way and went to him, collapsing beside the bed and burying her face in his shoulder.

"Oh, Paul! I'm sorry about last night. I didn't mean it, any of it!"

He turned her face so that she had to look at him. His face was very close to hers, his expression tender. "You are a silly cow, aren't you?" he said affectionately. "What did you have to get yourself in such a state for?"

"I don't know. I was stupid."

His arms went round her. "Hey, there's no need to start crying again, pea-brain. Come on. You shouldn't let it *matter* so much."

"I know," she sniffed. "I don't blame you for being angry with me. I don't know what got hold of me. I'm sorry."

He stroked her hair. "Let's forget it, shall we? The sun's shining and it's our day off."

"Mmm." She adapted to the sudden change of atmosphere. The day ahead stretched enticingly now, hours to fill with enjoyment. "What shall we do? Are you going to paint?"

"No, let's go out. Where do you want to go?"

"Let's get the ferry across the river and walk along the cliff path," she suggested, full of enthusiasm. "Take some sandwiches for lunch and stay out all day. And find a beach, and swim."

"OK." He lay back against the pillow, pulling her with him, and then he rolled her over and smiled down at her, his weight pinning her down. "But not yet."

Saturday and Sunday, 24/25 August

We had a great night. Everyone came in about the same time, quite late, and we decided to get a Chinese takeaway and then we stayed up for hours, drinking and playing music. Even Gillian came down, though she went to bed at about midnight. I've never heard Beano talk so much. He was really funny, telling jokes and doing Nixon impressions. And we smoked pot. It was the first time I'd had any but I wasn't going to say so. I don't know whether I inhaled it properly. It didn't make me feel high or anything, just relaxed and dreamy.

Paul's asleep now. If he can get off early tonight we're going to see *The Sting*.

Jess is quite friendly now. She and Bill are a bit fed up over how long the gallery is taking. I went round the other day and it doesn't look much like a gallery, more like a greengrocer's shop, which is what it was before. There isn't much space. They're about to start painting the walls so Paul and I might help. Ollie's coming down next week, with some other bloke.

Tuesday 27 August

Ill.

Wednesday 28 August

Ill.

Thursday 29 August

Ill, but getting better. I've got to recover for the weekend. It's my birthday on Saturday.

I told Paul about that batty woman next door and he said he'll chuck the empties in her front garden next time we have a party.

Abigail had begun to feel dizzy on Monday. On Tuesday morning she woke up with a pounding headache and a sore throat, and the room revolved slowly when she got to her feet.

"It's no good," she told Paul. "I can't go to work." She sat down heavily on the mattress and clutched her reeling head. "It feels like 'flu."

"Sure it's not a delayed hangover? That's what I felt like the other morning."

"No, it's definitely 'flu. I'll have to ask if I can use next door's phone to let Mrs T. know."

"I'll call in and tell her if you like, when I go to the pub at twelve," Paul said, rummaging in the heap of clothes for something to wear.

"God, no. She'd have a fit. I told her I was staying with relations."

"I'll say I'm your cousin then." Paul's search was proving fruitless. "Didn't you say you were going to the launderette yesterday?"

"I didn't feel well, I told you," Abigail reproached him. "You'll have to go yourself if you're out of clothes. No, I'll phone. She wouldn't believe you. She's a bit suspicious anyway."

"I'll have to wear yesterday's shirt again," Paul said, throwing dirty clothes about. "Where is it?"

"How should I know?" Abigail slid back into bed and closed her eyes. "It's there somewhere."

Paul put on a creased navy T-shirt and then went downstairs and brought her some tea before going off to help Bill and Jess with the painting. At nine, Abigail struggled out of bed, put on some clothes and went to the house next door. It had a pink crazy-paving path bordered by scarlet salvias – no colour sense, Abigail thought. She rang the bell, which played a jangly tune and prompted a small white dog to appear in the bay window, yapping wildly. The net curtain twitched back, briefly revealing a face, and then footsteps came to the door. The woman who stood there was fortyish, wearing a checked nylon overall over her clothes. Abigail had seen her going in and out with the fluffy dog but they had never spoken.

"Hello, I'm from next door," she said. "Do you think I could use your phone?" She held out her hand to show that she had the money ready. "I'm not well and I can't go to work today, and I need to let them know."

The woman recoiled as if Abigail had made an obscene suggestion.

"You've got a cheek," she shrilled in a voice to match the yapping dog's. "Bunch of hippies, turning the place into a slum. You're not setting foot in my house. Loud music, day and night . . . rubbish left to blow about the street . . . all of you on the dole, I suppose, scrounging off decent people . . ."

Completely taken aback, Abigail recovered enough to say, "But I'm not on the dole. I told you, I've got a job. That's why I need to make a phone call."

The woman took no notice. "This is a respectable street, or used to be. Decent people live here. Ill, are you? I'm not surprised. All of you living in sin. God knows what you get up to in there. Drugs, I've no doubt. If I had my way I'd turn the lot of you out on the streets. It's a disgrace. Use my phone, bringing who knows what filthy germs with you! You can think again."

She stepped back briskly and slammed the door in Abigail's face.

"Narrow-minded bigot!" Abigail yelled at the frosted glass, before marching away up the path, outraged and shaking. *Living in sin!* Did people really still think like that, behind their Persil-white net curtains? Abigail wouldn't be surprised if the woman came out to scour the doorstep as soon as she had gone, in case filthy contagion lurked there. Back on the pavement Abigail hesitated, not wanting to risk a similar tirade from the neighbour on the other side. She would have to walk to the public phone box three streets away.

By the time she got back she felt ready to collapse; the short walk had seemed like a fifteen mile hike. She hauled herself up to her room and sank into bed, not bothering to undress. Swallowing was painful and her head throbbed. She would have liked a hot drink, but felt too dizzy to go all the way downstairs again.

Eventually she slept. When she awoke much later, heavy-eyed and sluggish, the ceiling was pounding to the insistent bass rhythm of rock music from Beano's room overhead. Staring up, she almost thought she could see the discoloured plaster pulsing to the beat. The bass thump reverberated inside her head, hurting her ears. Muffling herself in pillows didn't help; the noise was captive inside her head, banging around to be let out.

She lay there miserably for a while. It was half-past twelve; Paul would be at the pub by now. She wanted sympathy and hot tea. Wallowing in self-pity, Abigail thought of being ill at home, in her own room. Mum would be in and out constantly, asking how she was, arranging the pillows comfortably, bringing drinks and throat sweets and Disprin and magazines, asking if she wanted anything from the library. Being ill at home, looked after and fussed over, suddenly seemed the most desirable thing imaginable. *I want my Mum*, she thought feebly.

She dozed again. Later, Paul came in, bringing her a welcome mug of tea before going back to the gallery with Bill.

"Is your sleeping bag here somewhere?" he asked, rummaging in the heap. "I think I'd better sleep downstairs tonight. I don't want to catch whatever you've got."

"In a roll behind that cardboard box." Abigail watched him pull it out. She felt hurt by his desertion, although it made sense.

She didn't see Paul again until next morning. The hours dragged past: dozing, waking, listening to the transistor radio, hearing the same news four times over. Around midday, desperate for something hot to soothe her throat, she went downstairs to the kitchen and met Gillian coming up.

"Are you all right?" Gillian said. "Paul said you weren't well but you really do look terrible!"

"I'm all right," Abigail said, and then, as Gillian continued to look at her in concern, "No, I'm not all right."

"Why are you out of bed, then?" Gillian turned her round and started to push her back up the stairs. "Go back to your room. What do you want, a cup of tea? I'll bring it to you."

Abigail submitted, and went back to bed. Slithering between the dingy sheets, she saw that the room really was a tip: when Paul searched for the sleeping bag he had scattered cassettes and carrier bags and dirty washing all over the floor, and Abigail hadn't had enough energy to do more than shove it together into a heap. Seeing it through Gillian's eyes, comparing it to the bright orderliness upstairs, she felt suddenly ashamed. She was wearing a nightdress with the sleeve half ripped off and her hair was greasy, hanging lankly over her face.

If Gillian was disgusted she showed no sign of it. She pushed the door open with her foot, holding a mug in each hand. "Here. Tea, and this is a herbal remedy – camomile and peppermint – to reduce your temperature. I suppose you haven't been to a doctor?"

"I haven't got a doctor. I haven't registered with one." Abigail sipped the tea gratefully, feeling it scald her raw throat. "Besides, they can't do anything for 'flu. They only tell you to rest and take aspirin."

"All the same, you ought to register. Can I get you anything else?"

"No, and thanks for this. But you could ask Beano to turn his music down. It's driving me insane."

Gillian smiled. "I know. It does get on your nerves. I have to turn mine up in competition. I'll be back later. Come up if you need anything."

Abigail sniffed the herbal drink and tried sipping it. It wasn't too bad. Better than going to a doctor, anyway; waiting in a room full of ill people always made her imagine she was breathing in masses of virulent germs. But Gillian was right; she ought to register with a doctor. Not for the 'flu, but because she hadn't done anything yet about getting herself on the Pill. She didn't fancy it much; the doctor would probably guess that she was Living in Sin and be disapproving about it. Perhaps a Family Planning Clinic would be better, if there were such a thing in Chilcombe Sands. She could ask Paul to go with her to lessen the ordeal, although she didn't really think he would agree. He hated illness and hospitals and all that sort of thing.

I'll do something about it next week, after I'm eighteen, she decided. I'll be a proper adult then and it won't be anybody else's business.

Saturday/Sunday, 31 August and 1 September

My birthday yesterday. We had a party on the beach and stayed out nearly all night. Everyone came. It was fantastic.

Beano had finished a painting. Abigail hadn't realized that he did any painting, having vaguely supposed that he lay on his bed all day deafening himself with Black Sabbath and Jimi Hendrix, but it seemed that he did paint and he had finished something. It was brought downstairs and put in the main room for everyone to admire: a vast square of Daler board, a savage creation of black and scarlet, apparently representing the beak and talons of some predatory bird clawing at the viewer out of the murky darkness. Abigail asked Beano if it had a symbolic meaning, but he said something incomprehensible in reply and wandered off, muttering to himself.

"This calls for a celebration," Bill said. He was in a holiday mood, because a delay with the wiring at the gallery had brought work to a standstill. "Beano's painting, Abby's birthday, and Ollie coming. Let's have a party."

It was a fine, calm evening, too perfect a summer evening for staying indoors. They piled into Paul's van and he drove a short distance along the coast, and then they carried their stuff down to the beach, beyond the cove where Paul and Abigail had gone on their first evening together. It was a spot popular with tourists in the daytime but far enough from the town to be deserted now that dusk was falling. The tide was low, the sound of the waves a distant murmur. Light spilled across the sea in a fading golden path from the west beneath purplish streaks of cloud; the sand gleamed, ribbed by the waves' retreat. Summer was passing now, the darkness closing in earlier. Soon the tourists would go, and the town would be left to its quiet overwintering.

Ollie and his friend Spike collected driftwood for a fire and spent a long time trying to light it with dried grass and twists of paper for kindling. "You can tell you two were never in the Boy Scouts," Bill said, dumping a crate of bottles in the sand. Everyone passed round bottles and cans, and when the fire had taken hold Jess produced beefburgers and sausages to cook on skewers and eat with chunks of French bread. Afterwards, greasy and sticky and sandy, Abigail wandered down to the tide's edge to wash. She watched her footprints filling with water and then rolled up her jeans and waded farther in. The tide was on the turn now, wavelets frilling at her ankles and then falling back, the sand gleaming faintly in the warm light. She looked back at her friends. The fire glowed beneath the darkness of the rocks, ringed round by dark figures, someone standing tall. Ollie was strumming his guitar; one of the others said something that sounded like the punch line of a joke, followed by ripples of laughter.

Overwhelmed by affection for them all, she walked back to join them, her feet sinking heavily into dry sand higher up the beach. They were smoking joints; the sweet resinous aroma hung in the air. Paul opened a beer can for Abigail, although she had already drunk enough cider to feel heady, and then passed her the joint he had been smoking. She stretched out in the sand beside him, totally content. She was wearing a new necklace he had given her for her birthday, a thong necklace with green stones which he had chosen because he said she should always wear green. She lay back in the sand looking up at the emerging stars and listening to Ollie's tuneless singing. From time to time Paul passed her the reefer and she smoked it lazily. The desultory voices of the others merged with the strummed guitar chords. Everything seemed sharp and clear, in spite of her headiness: the tiny points of stars piercing the dark silk cloth of sky, the crescent moon like something newly-sculpted, the rocks rearing in front of her. Fresh smells of salt breeze and woodsmoke and sand. Paul's hand in hers, the skin dry and warm, his fingers occasionally caressing hers. She could feel the ridges of bone under the skin, the blood pulsing where the vessels ran over bone at his wrist. It pleased her to share such a silent unnoticeable intimacy with him while he talked lazily to Beano.

Spike had taken over the guitar and was singing *Starry, starry night* in a tender crooning voice. Suddenly Abigail couldn't bear to lie still any longer. She wanted to take everything in with all her senses: the starry night, the sea, the faint breeze that stirred her hair and blew smoke into her eyes. She released Paul's hand and stood up. No one took any notice of her. Bill was lying with his head in Jess's lap, Gillian seemed to have gone, Beano was trying to resurrect the fire by poking it with a stick. Sparks flew upwards, fanning out, their golden specks of light dwindling as they merged with the colder stars. Abigail craned her neck to watch them, not quite steady on her feet.

She wondered where Gillian had gone. Perhaps to find driftwood for the fire. She would go and find her. She stumbled off, staying by the high-tide line until the pebbles and shells and dried seaweed hurt her feet, and then she forgot about Gillian and wandered closer to the sea. The soles of her feet could feel every ridge of the wave patterns on the sand, just as she had felt the ridgy tendons of Paul's wrist. The tide was reaching out to her, racing up the beach, the waves singing to her, calling her. She stubbed her toe painfully on a rock and realized that she had wandered close to the flat ledge and cave where Paul had brought her that first night. She giggled, because everything seemed funny. Now she must get into the sea, let it bathe her and soothe her and carry her away. She stripped off her clothes and laid them on a rock, and ran down to the wet slippery sand and on into the waves, splashing out until the weight of water stopped her from running, and then she flopped full length. The icy shock of the water washed over her shoulders, making her gasp. She began to swim, making stilted frozen circles with her arms, and then gradually thawing and loosening. It was like swimming in chilled wine. A warmer current carried her on a buoyant rush; her legs kicked free, there was no sand beneath her. She would swim out along the shimmering moon-path until she reached the moon itself . . .

"Abby! Abby!"

There was a voice inside her head, shouting. Paul's voice. He wanted to swim to the moon with her. She stretched out a hand to touch him, but her hand groped empty water. She listened again. Rolling over, she looked back towards the shore. A dark figure stood there, waving agitatedly.

"Abby! Come *back*, for God's sake!"

He wanted her. He must want to tell her something. Reluctantly she left the moon-path and swam back. The water felt warm now, sliding over her limbs like melted glass. She felt like a sea creature reaching unfamiliar land. Paul waded into the shadows and lunged towards her. She laughed, trying to pull him in so that he could float in moonlight with her. Much the stronger, he pulled her upright and clasped her against him and dragged her on to the sand. He wasn't laughing with her but his mouth was open, shouting, and words were coming out and then floating away into the waves' song.

And then, shouting in her ear, "Are you trying to kill yourself? Abby!" His voice was angry and scared, both at once. "What did you think you were doing? You could have drowned!"

She clung to him, suddenly dismayed by what she had done. She was frightened and cold, her skin prickling with gooseflesh, hair clinging damply to her shoulders. Paul's arms were round her; she was soaking him, but he wasn't angry any more. He held her close, warming her. "Abby! You fool! Do you realize what could have happened if I hadn't come to find you?"

"Yes. Yes. I'm sorry," she sobbed.

He gathered her wet hair into a tail and squeezed the water out of it, sending a rivulet down her back.

"Where are your clothes, pea-brain?"

"Up there. By the cave." She turned to point, unbalanced on her feet. Paul supported her, one arm round her, the other gripping her forearm, and they made their way slowly up the beach towards the black eyelet of the cave. She was chilled, limp as a dishcloth, her legs wavering. He seemed unsteady too, or perhaps it was the reeling in her own head that made her think they were lurching unsteadily rather than walking. She pointed again, and Paul groped for her clothes and started drying her with them.

"I'm so cold . . ."

She didn't know whether she had spoken the words or only thought them. His hands moved over her body, rubbing, mesmerizing. His face was close to hers; she could see a glimmer of reflected light in each eye. Shivering, she reached up a hand and ran it down his jaw where the skin was stubbly and unshaven, and then over his lips, tracing their firm shape. His breath was warm against her fingers. She slid her hand round his neck, under the thick hair.

"Oh, Paul . . . I'm sorry . . . I didn't mean . . ."

"It's all right. It's all right now." His voice was soothing, as if talking to a child. She closed her eyes and swayed, and he clutched at her and then somehow they weren't standing any more but sinking into the dry sand, the blackness of the cave mouth arching over them like a cathedral. His lips were against hers, tasting of salt, his tongue probing, and his hands ran down her body, sending shivers of warmth. She was carried along with the sudden surge of feeling, as helpless as driftwood on the tide. She tugged at his wet shirt, undoing the buttons with trembling fingers, and then his arms flailed as he thrust it off and flung it aside. He fumbled with the fastening of his jeans and she waited for him, lying back on the sand; her head swam, and the sky revolved slowly above her, the stars blurring. She could smell water on rock, and the sharp tang of seaweed. Paul murmured something and came back to her, his weight holding her down, to stop her from floating away. His lips moved over her face and neck, and she laced her fingers through his hair and clung to him as if he would slither out of her grasp like seaweed.

"I love you," she whispered. The words echoed in her head and swirled in the recesses of the cave and were swallowed.

Part Four

*N*ot long after that I wished Paul had left me to drown. I was desperate enough to wish that.

I tried to make excuses, blaming the circumstances, the excitement, the drink, a wish to impress Paul with my daring and eccentricity; I blamed everything except myself and my own stupidity.

It wasn't long before I realized. It seemed like the end of the world. I was panic-stricken; I wanted to hide, or run for help, or die, anything rather than face up to it. I was officially an adult now but I felt like a helpless child.

*　*　*　*　*

Wednesday 2 October

I'm so worried. Three weeks late, more than three weeks. I haven't said anything to Paul yet but every day I feel more desperate. How can we have let it happen? How can we have been so stupid? But how unlucky as well, if it turns out to be what I think. It's not fair! Just once without taking precautions, just *once*, and I think I might be pregnant. One slip and my whole life's turned upside down.

Pregnant. I've used that word now, written it down. I don't want to use it. I've tried to pretend everything's normal but then that awful word comes into my mind and now that it's there I can't shove it away out of sight.

Oh God. You can't do this to me.

Perhaps I'm not. Tonight, or tomorrow, my period will start. Mum always used to call it *the curse* and I thought that was funny and old-fashioned. But now it would be more of a blessing. I want it more than anything, I want the cramp and the pain and the bother. I want it so badly that I keep trying to imagine it.

What will I do? What will Paul say? How will I tell him?

I can't face it. I can't even think about it. I can't think ahead beyond tomorrow. Tomorrow everything will be all right, and I'll be able to laugh at myself for getting in such a state. I'll tear this page out and rip it up so that I don't even have to remember how frightened I am now. And then I'll go to the doctor and go on the Pill and not have to worry again.

Thursday 3 October

No change.

I'm going to have to tell Paul. I haven't said anything yet but he must have noticed how oddly I'm behaving. Too wrapped up in my fears to take much notice of him, even to listen to what he says.

I ought to tell him. It's his worry too. But I can't think how to put it.

The season was starting to feel autumnal. A gusty, showery day, a touch of coldness in the wind. Abigail huddled into her jacket and wished she had worn a warmer jumper. This is what winter will be like, she thought: the seafront almost deserted, the wind whipping up the waves, the sea pressing against the shore, grey and sullen, crunching and rolling the pebbles. A discarded fish-and-chips wrapper gusted along the concrete; in the shelter the wind flapped a torn corner of a poster. A woman with a tartan shopping-trolley plodded along the promenade towards Abigail, facing into the wind. A local, not a holiday-maker. Soon the tourists would be gone. Already the family on the beach, wrapped up in anoraks and doggedly eating a picnic, seemed like intruders. They would pack up their buckets and spades and return to suburbia, jobs and school.

Intruders, but not as much as the thing growing inside me, Abigail thought. A tiny, microscopic thing, a combination of cells, a perverse thing that's chosen to lodge and grow there. Splitting and growing. A time bomb. Such a fragile, helpless thing, the result of chance and bad luck, bad timing and stupidity – it *can't*, it can't survive! No one asked for it, no one wants it – go away, go away and give me my body back, for myself.

She could think about nothing else but could still hardly believe it. Her tightest jeans had zipped up as smoothly as ever over her flat stomach. There are other reasons for missing a period, she told herself. There's no proof. I couldn't be so unlucky.

But she was losing her hold, her sense of having changed into someone different. Her relaxed summer self was fading with the lazy evenings of sunlight and the long shadows across the beach. The frightened child had crept back, afraid of getting things wrong, afraid of being found out. She was the nervous first-year at grammar school who worried in case she couldn't tell whether 2x was more or less than 3y, or got told off for forgetting to change into her indoor shoes. The girl who shrank into a corner of the sweaty changing-room, fumbling her poplin blouse off and her Aertex shirt on as quickly as she could, so that the others wouldn't notice she didn't wear a bra yet. The girl whose first time out with a boy, Philip Gladwin from the boys' school, had petrified her because she didn't know how to kiss properly. Hide, run away, keep quiet, do what everybody else does, don't let anyone see.

Don't be daft, she mocked herself; you're older now, an adult. You've grown out of all that. None of those things was as terrible as you thought; the problems of one day were forgotten by the next, just as this will be. She had come to an involuntary standstill outside Drake's Drum, and she stood there thinking of Paul at the bar, pulling pints or washing glasses in his unhurried way. His movements were always lithe and fluid, suggesting athleticism although he took no exercise beyond an occasional swim or a walk to the pub. She immediately felt warmer and less alone, picturing the way he would turn to her with a sudden pleased smile if she went in. She didn't have to face it on her own. Paul was there and he never worried. There was always some easy solution, or things would sort themselves out without intervention. Paul would comfort her and tell her she was a silly cow to get herself worked up, and tomorrow her period would start and they would both laugh about their near miss. They loved each other and nothing mattered beyond that.

The temptation to see him was so strong that she had her hand on the pub's front-door handle before turning back.

It was no good. Not now. She couldn't tell him while he was at work, and not being able to tell him would make her morose and silent. She went instead to the iron railings around the harbour wall. Even inside the harbour's cradling arm, the wind beat up waves and made the moored boats rock and sway, their cables clinking. The yachting people were in retreat, shrouded in yellow rainwear and appearing only briefly to adjust a rope or look at the weather before disappearing below for mugs of tea. They would soon be gone like migrating swifts, leaving the harbour to the dour fishing smacks and the shabby dinghies. Abigail shivered. Her hair was tied back in the ponytail required by Mrs T.'s decorum, but the wind whipped strands loose and lashed them against her face. It was too cold to stay here but too early to go to the café. She had come to walk and think, but it was too cold to walk, too agonizing to think, and she still had no idea how to tell Paul. She remembered a scene in an old black-and-white film: "Darling, I've something wonderful to tell you. Can you guess what it is?" But this wasn't wonderful. It was a disaster, an earth-shattering disaster. "Darling,

I've got something dreadful to tell you . . ." No. Tell him straight. "Paul, I think I'm pregnant." How would he react?

I'll do it tonight, she told herself, and turned her back to the wind. No matter what.

She couldn't find her diary when she went to bed, and it worried her. It was always in exactly the same place under the mattress so that she could slip a hand underneath and pull it out, anonymous in its plain black covers. It wasn't there now. She couldn't exactly remember replacing it last time she had written in it, but keeping it secret from Paul was so automatic that she could not imagine absent-mindedly putting it somewhere else. She searched her bag, the windowsill and among the few books they possessed, but without success.

She worried about it for a while, waiting for Paul. What she was going to say to him was far more important than a mislaid diary. She could hear Beano moving about in the room above, and once she heard Gillian's quick light tread down the top stairs to the bathroom and up again. What would Gillian, with her orderly self-contained world, think of her now? Would she sympathize, or would she be scornful of anyone who could get herself into such a predicament?

In spite of leaving the light and radio on to keep herself awake, she was dozing when Paul returned. Half-asleep, she heard him clomping up the stairs and then he came into the room. She opened her eyes to find him looking down at her with an odd expression. He didn't seem to be in a particularly good mood. Her heart sank. It wasn't going to be easy. Saying nothing, he pulled his clothes off and threw them down in the corner. She watched as he moved naked towards the light switch. He was obviously going to get into bed without washing, which he often did when tired or irritable. His body was skinny and lithe, his arms thin, ribs showing above the hollowed stomach; anyone would consider him undernourished if they didn't see the amount of food he put away. He had the boyish lankiness of an adolescent, and yet he was man enough to have brought about this awful, cataclysmic, unseen change in her own body. She looked at his set face and wondered for the first time whether he had guessed.

"Leave the light on for a minute," she said suddenly, wanting to see his expression when she told him.

"What for?"

The guarded look on his face aroused her suspicions and she immediately connected it with the missing diary. When she didn't answer, he shrugged and said, "You can get out and turn it off yourself, then." He got into bed, not touching her, and pulled the sheets up.

"Did you find a black notebook under the bed?" she asked.

"No!"

His reply was too quick; she knew it was a lie. He had found it, and no doubt read it.

"You did, didn't you?" she persisted. "Where is it now?"

Paul huffed impatiently and jerked the sheets up to his ears. "It's there under the mattress. You can't have looked properly."

"What were you looking under the mattress for?"

"For God's sake, what is this? The Spanish Inquisition? I wasn't looking. I was going to take the sheets to the launderette. You nag at me often enough to take my turn."

"But the sheets haven't been washed. What stopped you going?"

He didn't reply, but she realized what had happened: he had found the diary and read it, and after that going to the launderette was the last thing on his mind.

"You read it, didn't you?" she said. "You know!"

"Yes, I bloody well read it!" With one impatient bound he was out of bed, opening the door. For a crazy moment she thought he was going to walk out of the house and into the street, naked as he was, but the sound of bare feet on lino stopped along the landing, and a door slammed. Abigail scrambled out of bed and lifted the sagging mattress. There was the diary, shoved to the middle, farther than she would have pushed it. She hooked it back and clasped it to her chest. As if it mattered any more. She felt doubly violated: her body, by this terrible thing, and now her secrets exposed too. A wave of self-pity engulfed her as she waited for him to come back. He shouldn't be like this! He shouldn't be remote and prickly, not now that he knew. It wasn't only her fault. He should have taken her in his arms and told her that everything would be all right, that he loved her and would look after her . . .

Along the landing the lavatory flushed. Abigail pushed the diary under the bed, as if there were still some point in hiding it. Paul came in, stony-faced, not looking at her. Her indignation clogged her throat and pulsed in her head. Why was it up to her to be tactful, to apologize? She felt like hitting him.

"Well, then?" she said, more harshly than she intended.

"Well what?"

"You *know* what I mean! You read it! I'm pregnant and I don't know what to do! Don't pretend it's all my fault! Tell me what you think, talk to me!"

He was back in bed, the light still on. He lay back with his arms bent up, fingers laced behind his head. Remote and disapproving, like a stranger.

"What do you expect me to think?" he said

coldly. "I'm not dancing about with delight, I can tell you that much. I told you to get yourself fixed up with the Pill, didn't I?"

"I was going to –"

He gave a contemptuous snort. "Fat lot of good that is now."

"What about you?" she demanded. "I didn't notice you offering to come with me to the Family Planning Clinic. Oh no. Nothing to do with you, I suppose." Her voice wavered. Any moment now she would burst into tears, and she knew him well enough by now to know that tears would only make him more impatient.

He looked at her directly for the first time. "Look, are you sure? How late is it?"

"Three weeks, nearly four. I mean no, I'm not sure. I haven't been to a doctor or anything. But what else can it be?"

"Jesus *Christ*." He hissed the word out. "That's all we need."

Hot angry tears welled up. "You're no help at all. I've had all these days of worry, because I didn't want to bother you, and now you're treating me as a nuisance, as if you had nothing to do with it . . ." She fumbled in her bag for a tissue.

"All right, all right," Paul said in a gentler tone. "You've having a rough time." He reached out for her arm and patted it absently, staring at the ceiling as if working something out. Eventually he said, "Look. We'll have to find out where you can go to get rid of it. How much it'll cost. I'll help you find the money."

"You'll *help* me . . ." She flung back the bedclothes and stood up. "Very decent of you, I'm sure, to help me out of my little problem. It's *our* responsibility, not just mine! Don't be so bloody-minded! How can you . . . act as if I'm some useless burden? Some charity appeal?"

"Don't get hysterical," he said sharply. "There's no point letting the whole house know." He pulled at her hand to make her sit down again. "Listen. I'm just trying to be practical. If you're – if we're in this mess then we've got to get out of it damn quick. Get rid of it."

She started to cry softly. "It's all right for you . . . Get rid of it, you say. It's not like putting rubbish out in the dustbin," she sniffed. "Have an abortion, that's what you mean. Why don't you say it?"

He looked at her. "Well, it's obvious. What else is there to do?"

"It's all right for you," she flared at him. "For you it's just a question of finding the money. I'm the one who'll have to go through with it. Have you thought what it's like, having an abortion?"

"There's no alternative, is there? I don't suppose it's pleasant, but—"

"Of course there's an alternative," she snapped.

His eyes widened. "You don't mean you're thinking of *having* the damn thing? A baby, for God's sake? You must be crazy. Forget that, Abby, forget that right away."

"I don't know what I'm thinking," she burst out. "I don't know. Only that you're not being much help. You don't care about *me*, do you? Only about not being lumbered . . ."

"Of course I do, stupid." He pulled her arm so that she half-fell against him and he put both arms round her. She submitted, desperate for comfort. He pulled the crumpled bedclothes up and tucked them around her, as if she were a child. He said softly, "Tomorrow it'll all seem different. Perhaps it's a false alarm. If it's not, we'll decide what to do. Go to sleep now."

She wanted to believe him, on all counts.

Friday 4 October

Oh God. It's even worse than it was before. How could he *do* this to me?

"Bye, then."

"Goodbye, dear. See you tomorrow."

Six o'clock. Mrs Trelawney was having a last fuss round, straightening a crooked picture, placing a flower vase in the exact centre of a table. Abigail went outside, wondering whether Paul might be waiting for her; he wasn't working at the pub today, and she hoped he might meet her for a drink or something to eat. But there was no sign of him. She started to walk home by herself.

She was turning over the new words in her vocabulary. They had always been there, available for use, but floating out of range, the property of other people. Now they demanded to be noticed and considered and used. Pregnant. Baby.

Abortion.

The word reminded her of social studies lessons at school: discuss the arguments for and against abortion. Even then, the word had alarmed her, with its associations of unnatural interference, brutal jettisoning. Now it was more than a discussion to be voted on at the end of the lesson, or written up for grading by a bored teacher who had seen the same arguments paraded in countless identikit essays. It was there in front of her, a terrifying doorway she would have to pass through if she wanted her normal life back.

She reacted instinctively against the idea of handing over her body to be probed and emptied, as if the thing inside her was a parasite. But wouldn't it be worth it for the glorious freedom of being herself again, the freedom everyone else took for granted?

Another day of worrying. Another day which could have brought an end to her ordeal, but obstinately refused to. She kept trying to conjure the dull ache of a period pain but her body would not oblige. Even worse, she had felt sick this morning when she first woke up. She hadn't dared tell Paul.

I shall have to go to a doctor, she thought; then at least I'll know the worst. Better to know definitely than to carry on with this useless hoping . . .

She reached Princeton Terrace and walked past the scrubbed front doorsteps and the autumnal gardens. What would that awful woman say, if she knew? . . . *immoral, living in sin, an unmarried mother on top of everything else* . . . Abigail imagined herself walking along the terrace, heavily pregnant, the net curtains twitching to reveal outraged faces . . .

But that was the least of her worries. The neighbours could think what they liked. She wanted to remind Paul that he'd once mentioned getting a place of their own. However things turned out, it would be nice to get away from their present squalor: the greasy kitchen, the inevitable sinkful of burnt saucepans, the bath which nobody cleaned. With the tourist season ending, it shouldn't be too difficult to find a flat or a bedsit. She would mention it to him tonight . . .

She let herself in and went upstairs. No one was around downstairs, but the customary thump of Beano's heavy rock reverberated through the floorboards. She remembered that Paul's van hadn't been parked outside in the street, and wondered where he was.

She realized as soon as she opened the door to their room.

Paul had gone.

Everything of his had been taken away, apart from a few squeezed-out paint tubes scattered on the floor. He had taken all his dirty clothes which had been stuffed into a dustbin bag, and the clean clothes heaped in the corner. His transistor radio, his art books and magazines. His records and his sleeping bag and his electric razor. Everything.

Stupid with shock, Abigail stared around the room, unable to believe what she saw. There must be some mistake. He was playing a trick on her, hiding somewhere. Her legs gave way and she slumped on the mattress, looking at her own heaped belongings, which suddenly looked pathetic and abandoned. Just as she felt. He had gone. Left her. Ditched her. Done a moonlight flit. Only not in moonlight, but on an ordinary Friday afternoon.

* * * *

Saturday 5 October

I'm on my own now. I'm going to have to get used to it.

How could he do this to me? How could he even think of it? I keep asking myself but there's no answer. Only the one I don't want to hear. He didn't care about me at all. He doesn't care.

I can't sleep and I feel like a wreck. It keeps going round and round in my head, getting nowhere. He doesn't love me. I suppose he never did. I've been fooling myself. Even now I keep thinking he's going to come back, he only went away for a weekend or something. I know it's stupid but I want him to come back so that I can hit him and throw things at him and scream, and tell him what a bastard he is. A selfish, thoughtless, self-centred, pig-headed, ignorant, lazy, cruel, unreliable, cowardly, lying bastard.

But he doesn't care what I think. He's definitely gone for good.

He left £25 in an envelope on the windowsill. I thought it was a letter, an explanation. What? "I'm sorry, I don't love you. I don't want any more to do with you. Sort out your own problems." But there wasn't even a note. Just the money. I don't know if it was the £25 for his car tax and he left it by mistake, or whether he left it on purpose. It seems like buying me off, settling his account. Perhaps he thought it would pay for an abortion. I've no idea how much it costs, or whether you can get it on the National Health. I know abortion's not illegal any more but I bet you can't get one just by asking. I don't want to think about it. I'm so frightened.

I keep going over everything he said, the night before last. It's obvious now. He was planning his escape.

What's he doing now? Who's he with?

It's all right for him, isn't it? He can clear off and forget all about it, the Thing. It's half his fault but he can run away, pay me off and leave me to cope. Or not cope. It's so unfair. I HATE HIM, I HATE HIM, I HATE HIM!

What am I going to do?

It was nearly eight in the morning but the house was quiet, as if everyone was still asleep. From habit, Abigail pushed her diary back into its hiding place before realizing that there was no need to. She lay back on the double mattress which now seemed far too big. Paul's absence was like a tangible thing, a silence pressing down on her, stifling her. She could smell him on the sheets, which were still crumpled and unwashed; it was all he had left of himself, his smell, and the Thing growing inside her. Today she would go to the launderette and wash his smell away, try to get rid of him. If only everything were as simple, and she could wash the rest of him away as cleanly as he'd disposed of her . . .

Someone went downstairs and she heard a clattering of saucepans in the kitchen. She didn't want to see anyone but she had to find out what the others knew about Paul; she would have preferred to talk to Bill, but it was Jess in the kitchen, standing at the sink. Her hair was unbrushed and she wore an outsize sweater with apparently nothing on underneath.

"God, this place is a mess," she complained, without turning round as Abigail approached. "Doesn't anyone ever think of clearing up after themselves?"

That was rich, coming from Jess, who never washed up until there wasn't a clean spoon or saucepan to be found. Abigail could have made a pointed retort if she'd been less desolate.

Jess turned to look for a tea-towel, dripping water all over the floor from the saucepan she was holding. She looked at Abigail in surprise. Abigail hadn't looked at herself in a mirror but she knew that her eyes must be red and puffy from crying.

"Here." She passed Jess a grimy tea-towel from the top of the cooker. Jess made no comment but bent down to rummage noisily in a cupboard, finding a place for the saucepan.

"You know Paul's left?" Abigail said to her crouched back.

Jess looked up at her. "Yes. He told me you were splitting up, you and him." She spoke as if it were a matter of no more than passing interest to either of them. She turned the hot tap on and held her hand under the trickle, and said, "Blast, there's no hot water. Didn't you put the boiler on last night?"

"It was the last thing I thought of," Abigail said impatiently.

"I suppose you're upset," Jess said, not unkindly. "But you should know Paul by now. He never sticks at anything for long. If you want the truth, I was surprised when he agreed to you coming down here."

"How do you mean?"

"Cosy twosomes aren't really his thing." Jess started to scrub at a scrambled-egg-encrusted saucapan. "If you hadn't been so keen on coming he'd never have agreed."

"But—" Abigail stared at her in confusion. "You've got it all wrong! Is that what he told you? And he even said we'd *agreed* to split up, as if we'd sat down and had a calm discussion about it—" There was a catch in her voice, and ready tears threatened. She wasn't going to cry in front of Jess. She swallowed and put out three mugs for the tea before speaking again with studied nonchalance. "Did he say where he was going?" She had already worked out that Paul wouldn't go home; he would probably expect her to return to her own parents, pregnant and helpless, and then he would be in trouble. "Was he going to Glasgow after all?"

Jess turned in surprise. "Glasgow? Why on earth would he go to Glasgow?"

"You know. To do his degree. At the College of Fine Art. Didn't he mention it?"

Jess laughed. "Told you he had a place at Glasgow, did he? That's a good one. He'd have mentioned it all right."

"How do you know he—" Abigail didn't know whether she was defending Paul or herself.

"He hasn't got a place at Glasgow, or anywhere else," Jess told her. "Because for one, he was too damned lazy to bother applying, and two, he knows he isn't good enough."

"Oh, but he—" Abigail's mind raced, trying to assimilate it all. What other lies had Paul told? What had she believed? She looked wildly at Jess, hoping she would say it was all a joke, a mistake, and that Paul wasn't really like that at all. Anger fizzed through her, a futile stinging anger that was powerless to hurt anyone other than herself.

"How much painting did you see him doing while he was here?" Jess continued. "He only scraped through his Foundation year by doing the bare minimum at the last minute. He liked being an art student for a year – trying it out. But he certainly wasn't even considering a degree course. It'd be too much like hard work, even if he got a place."

"I thought he was your friend. How can you talk about him like that?" Abigail retaliated, annoyed by Jess's assumption that she knew best.

Jess shrugged. "Sure, he's my friend. That doesn't make him perfect. He's Paul – he comes and goes as he pleases. Doesn't bother me."

"But he's let you down too. He was going to stay here all year, help you with the gallery—" Abigail faltered, realizing that this was another myth of Paul's. He had helped at the gallery no more than three or four times, and had taken no part in the planning. Slowly it dawned on her that he had used Bill and Jess as providers of cheap accommodation, herself as a tolerable companion, provided she wasn't a nuisance.

Jess didn't seem to mind. She only said, "Well, he did a bit." She looked at Abigail more closely and said, "There's no point getting in a state about it. It was fun while it lasted, wasn't it? Things don't last for ever. Have you made the tea? I'm parched."

Abigail found the tea bags in the cupboard. "Where do you think he's gone?"

"Bumming round Europe, he said. He was

going to drive to Poole and get the ferry to Cherbourg."

"On his own?" Abigail said sharply, thinking of Claudia. She had tried not to be suspicious of Claudia since that first disastrous row, but now she pictured Claudia standing with Paul on the open deck of the Cherbourg ferry, her blonde hair streaming in the wind. Paul and Claudia setting off into the freedom of a new country, like the *Easy Rider* film. Paul and Claudia in some romantically rustic French hotel, checking into their room, laughing. Making love. Claudia wouldn't be so stupid as to let herself get pregnant. She wouldn't let Paul get bored with her and throw her away like a worn garment.

"He didn't say," Jess said. She took a milk bottle out of the fridge and sniffed the contents. "Just about usable."

Abigail suddenly felt unbearably weary, her anger gone. She was exhausted with worry and lack of sleep; her lids were heavy and the daylight hurt her eyes. What did it matter whether Paul had gone with Claudia or with anyone else? He had hurt her terribly, but he couldn't do any more to hurt her now.

Jess poured out the tea and said, "I suppose you'll be clearing off as well? Aren't you going back to college?"

"No, I packed it in. I need to get a job. The café shuts down soon for the winter."

Winter. The thought of it sent a shiver down Abigail's spine. Winter in a cosy room with Paul was one thing. Winter on her own – long dark evenings in the chill of unrelieved squalor – was another. And getting a proper job wasn't going to be easy, not if she were really pregnant. Jess didn't know about that part of it, of course. That was one thing Paul hadn't bothered to tell her.

"Want some toast?" Jess offered. "I'm making some for Bill and me."

Abigail was feeling slightly sick again and would have liked some toast to settle her stomach, but she was too preoccupied with her multiplying problems to think of eating. There was a mushroom cloud rising over her, spreading, contaminating everything; the starting point not a split atom, but a fusion of two cells. Such a tiny, insignificant thing.

"I suppose it's not the ideal time to mention it," Jess said, looking around for matches to light the grill, "but you do realize you're going to have to pay Paul's rent as well as your own, don't you, if you want to keep the room?"

Tuesday 8 October

I did two positive things today. I went to the doctor, and I went to the library.

It was a man doctor, of course. I asked for the woman, but she's away for a fortnight. So it had to be the man. I'd go mad if I waited another two weeks.

He was all tweedy, quite old and a bit teacherish. Going in, I felt as if this strange man could put everything right for me, just because he's a doctor. Take these pills and everything will be all right in the morning.

But he can't, of course. The first thing he said was that the most likely reason for missing a period is being pregnant, especially for a healthy girl my age. He asked whether I'd had unprotected sex and I felt like a silly kid who didn't know how pregnancies happen. Then he asked about my boyfriend and whether we were going to get married. I wanted to shout out, Married! You must be joking! I haven't even got a boyfriend any more. It was as much as I could do to get an answer out. I expect he thought, here's another silly girl who's got herself into trouble. Which is exactly what I am.

He took my blood pressure and listened to my heart and told me I seem perfectly healthy. That was the last thing I wanted to hear. I'd have preferred him to find something seriously wrong with me, anything to make it less likely I'm pregnant.

Now I've got to get a urine sample and wait for the result of a test. I hate all that sort of thing. Doctors, clinics, injections. It makes me feel like an object instead of a person.

Then I got a book out of the library about pregnancy, and smuggled it indoors. That made me feel even worse, all those pictures of bloated women. That isn't going to happen to me! I'm not going to let myself turn into a great clumsy whale! And it keeps going on about *your husband.* "You and your husband will have so much to discuss at this special time," that sort of puke-making thing. I threw it across the room.

All my hopes are hanging on one word. Negative. Someone will tell me the result and it will be negative. It'll be like being let out of a cage.

Friday 11 October

Bumped into Claudia today. She hasn't gone with Paul after all. I've changed my mind about her completely. It was all my imagination before, anyway. A lot of things were just my imagination.

Abigail was in the High Street, looking for the ABC Secretarial Agency at number 58. Number 50 was a mother-and-baby shop; she couldn't help looking at the window display of carrycots and baby-bouncers, tiny boots and shoes, baby clothes in primary-colour stripes or soft pastel knitting. The door bell jangled as she passed and a young pregnant woman came out leading a toddler by the hand. Abigail stopped to let them out and the mother smiled her thanks. She looked happy and relaxed, the textbook picture of a contented mother-to-be. Radiant, was the word the library book used. *You may be filled with a radiant sense of wellbeing*. If I'm radiating anything, Abigail thought, it's anger, and sheer blind terror. It must be easy to be radiant if you're going home to a comfortable house and a kind husband.

"Abby! Abby!"

Someone was shouting at her across the street and she turned to see, of all people, Claudia. In her imagination Claudia was in France, sipping Pernod in a pavement café and attracting male glances, or strolling along a boulevard hand-in-hand with Paul. But here was Claudia, waiting for a gap in the traffic and darting across the road. She wore a grey duffel coat with a guernsey sweater underneath and looked quite ordinary, not the irresistibly desirable girl she had become in Abigail's fantasy.

"I thought it was you," she said breathlessly. "How is Paul? I have been worried about him since he hasn't been coming in to work. I thought perhaps he is ill but there is no message from him."

"No, he's not ill," Abigail said. "He's gone."

"Gone?" Claudia's blue eyes expressed concern. "You and he have parted company?"

"Yes. He's gone to France, I think."

Claudia frowned. "He said nothing to the landlord about leaving. He is very annoyed, Mike. He goes once to Paul's house but found no one there. And there is no phone. You are staying on here?"

"Yes. There's nowhere else for me to go."

"Me, I go home to Germany this week." Claudia glanced at her watch. "Are you in a hurry? Shall we have some coffee?"

They went to Pizzaland, the nearest place. Abigail led the way to the table where she had sat with Paul on her first evening, as if to defy him. If anyone had told me first thing this morning that I'd be having coffee with Claudia, she thought, I'd have laughed, or imagined myself flying at her in a fury. Instead she felt positively grateful to Claudia for not having run off with Paul; for having been let down by him, in a small way.

They ordered their coffee. Claudia said, "You have known Paul a long time?"

"No, not long. A few months." Abigail felt suddenly weary of Paul. The ache of misery was there inside her but she didn't have to think about it every minute of the day. "Let's talk about something else. Where in Germany do you live?"

"Berlin. I am going home there to continue my studies. I am looking forward very much to being at home with my family. I miss them."

"Berlin? Behind the Iron Curtain?"

"Yes. I was born there. My parents are both Berliners. It is a strange place in many ways, but I have known nothing else." She told Abigail about the Wall and Checkpoint Charlie, and Unter den Linden. Listening, Abigail remembered that Berlin had been bombed by the RAF during the war. Night after night the big bombers had flown out to destroy it, and hundreds of aircrew had died in the attempt. Both Abigail's parents had worked on the same airfield in Lincolnshire, and she remembered now that someone Mum knew had died on one of the raids; her father had told her about it. Although doubting that this was the most tactful subject to raise, she mentioned it to Claudia.

"Yes. There was much terrible suffering on both sides," Claudia said, "but now the ruins are rebuilt and we are able to sit here and talk as friends."

She wore a gold chain round her neck with a small engraved medallion which hung outside the collar of her guernsey sweater and caught the light as she moved. Noticing it, Abigail remembered the gold locket her mother wore, and the strand of dark hair it contained. The connection between this and what she had just been thinking about came to her as the solution to a puzzle. Why hadn't it occurred to her before? Perhaps the locket had been given to Mum by the man who died in the Berlin raid. If so, they must have been more to each other than just friends; people didn't give gold lockets or strands of hair to casual friends. So Mum had had a lover before Dad and presumably she would have married him if he hadn't been killed. Did that make Dad second best, a consolation? This glimpse of the past intrigued her so much that she wished she could ask Mum about it, to know whether her theory was right, and to find out more. But of course that was impossible.

Claudia was talking about the psychology degree she was going to take. "You are a student also?" she asked Abigail.

"No. I need a job."

"There will be a vacancy at the pub now I am going," Claudia said. "I remember that you would have liked it before."

Abigail flushed in embarrassment, remembering how hostile she had been to Claudia at their first meeting.

"No, I need a full-time job. Secretarial work would pay better. I need to earn some money."

"You are not close to your family?" Claudia said.

Abigail shook her head dumbly, not trusting herself to speak about her family. Their eyes met, and Claudia said, "That is a pity. You are very lonely, I think, now that Paul has gone."

Her foreignness seemed to make it possible for her to say such direct things. Abigail nodded, and Claudia said, "Are you free tomorrow night? If so, there is a party at the pub, a goodbye party for me. I would be very pleased if you came."

"Thank you," Abigail said, pleased with this unexpected gesture of friendship. "I'd like to."

Sunday 13 October

I enjoyed it last night in the pub. Claudia's made loads of friends here and they were all there to see her off. She gave me her address in Berlin and wants us to keep in touch. It's a pity I've only just made friends with her. I was stupid to think of her as a rival. Paul wasn't worth competing for anyway.

Monday 14 October

I'm a failure. I might as well face up to it. I've failed at everything I've tried to do. I failed with Paul, I've got nowhere with my idea of being an artist. I've thrown away everything I ever had, for nothing. I can't even get a boring office job. I always thought I'd have that to fall back on.

The ABC Secretarial Agency was above an optician's, reached by a dark and narrow flight of stairs. There was only one person inside, a woman with grey hair and mauve-rimmed glasses, who sat at a big wooden desk with boxes of index cards on it. It was nothing like Abigail's original idea of temping: going into West End branches of Alfred Marks or Brook Street Bureau to take her pick from dozens of glamorous jobs. Glamour didn't even feature on her list of priorities any more. Money and security headed the list.

She had to fill in a form first. She listed her O-levels and her Typewriting Stage 1, gave a generous estimation of her shorthand and typing speeds and invented a full-time job at Fox Motors to enter under *Previous Employment*.

"No actual shorthand qualifications," the woman observed. "I shall have to give you a shorthand-typing test. Pen or pencil?" She handed Abigail a lined notepad and a choice of writing implements.

Not having expected this, Abigail wished she had thought of practising. She was hopelessly rusty. The woman picked up a stop-watch and rattled off, "Dear Sir, We are in receipt of your letter and remittance of the 20th September, and wish to advise you that we have acted in accordance with your instructions . . ."

The pace was too fast for Abigail to note down more than half of it. She was shown to a big old-fashioned typewriter at a desk in a corner, where all her powers of invention could not supply the missing words and phrases. The woman shook her head over the result.

"I'm sorry, Miss Fox. Your shorthand's simply not up to scratch. I'm afraid I can't possibly offer you work as a shorthand typist or secretary. I might be able to find you some copy-typing or filing, but the rates would be lower."

"What have you got?" Abigail asked desperately.

The woman flicked through the card index on her desk. "We're coming to a quiet time of year. There's one in Taunton, but that's rather a long way to travel. You don't drive, I suppose?"

Abigail shook her head.

"That's no use, then. One here at the bank, but they did specify over twenty, and as you haven't had much previous experience I doubt whether you'd suit. I'll take up a reference anyway—" she glanced at Abigail's form – "from Fox Motors. Same name – is that a family business?"

"No, it's just a coincidence," Abigail lied. "And anyway they've closed."

"Pity. A good reference would have helped with placements." Flick, flick. The painted fingernail dismissed each card in turn. "Nothing very promising, but I'll make a few enquiries today and ring you at home. Oh, you're not on the phone? Perhaps you could call in tomorrow, then." The card-box snapped shut, closing the lid on Abigail's hopes. "Late afternoon would be best."

Tomorrow. Tomorrow I get the result of the pregnancy test, and it will be another world.

Tuesday 15 October
Positive.

Positive. The word sounded in her ears like a death sentence. Positive. Pregnant. It was official now; there was no escaping it. Her last veil of hope had been snatched away.

"Come and sit down, Abigail. This is a tremendous shock for you, obviously." The nurse showed her into a separate consulting room. She was young, kind and concerned, ready with advice and sympathy. Abigail looked at her and at the proffered seat, aghast. If she sat down for a cosy chat she would erupt into hysterical tears. She couldn't stay here.

Turning, she sprinted for the door and closed it firmly behind her, catching a glimpse of the nurse's dismayed face. Out into the corridor, startling an elderly couple at the receptionist's hatch. Out into the street, skittering round pedestrians, running past the shops. She almost expected the nurse and the tweedy doctor to give chase, dragging her back for sympathy and advice. She didn't want sympathy or advice. She wanted to escape, run away, as if she could leave her pregnancy behind in the consulting room.

But she couldn't run for ever. Slowing, she gasped for breath, while her surroundings came into focus. Opposite her was the optician's and the ABC Agency, and she remembered that she was supposed to call back there this afternoon. She climbed the stairs in a semi-trance and stared wildly at the woman inside.

Mrs ABC, as Abigail thought of her, must have attributed her dishevelled state to desperation for a job. She said, "It's all right, Miss Fox. I've found you something." She handed over a printed sheet. Abigail read, *Claims Department, South Devon Insurers. Contact: Mr P. Maltravers. Hours: 9–5.30.*

"If you suit them, there may be a few months' work available, to cover a maternity leave. So do your best to be reliable."

Abigail put the form into her bag, hardly listening to the instructions about tax forms and pay claims. *Maternity leave!* She almost laughed out loud. *She* was going to need maternity leave unless something happened. Outside on the pavement she looked at the form again and read it properly. At least she had a proper job now. A job, and money: not a fortune, it would work out at about fifteen pounds a week, but more than she got from the café.

She would have to tell Mrs T. she wasn't coming back next week. It was short notice, but Abigail couldn't help that. The Harbour Lights Café would be closing for the winter soon.

Positive. Pregnant. The words revolved around her head. It was like a label stamped on her forehead for everyone to read; she had to remind herself that no one else actually knew. Except the doctor and nurse. They had her address and she wondered whether they would try to contact her there. It was another reason for moving out, quickly: no one must know.

There was a bedsit advertised in this week's local paper. She had written down the phone number and decided to ring now from the post office. She desperately wanted to be on her own, away from anyone who knew her. Part of her mind acknowledged that she would be lonely and frightened, but she pushed these thoughts away. She had to move out. Bill and Jess and Beano were Paul's friends, not hers; they didn't want her.

Abortion. Abortion. You'll have to have an abortion, a voice chanted in her head, in rhythm with her footsteps.

I can't. I'm too much of a coward. I can't bear the thought of handing myself over, a passive lump to be poked at.

What else are you going to do? At least it'll soon be over that way. It won't be pleasant but you'll have to put up with it.

I can't. I just can't.

What's the use of sorting out jobs and flats if you're going to swell up like a balloon within a couple of months? Who's going to want you then?

No one wants me now.

Stop wallowing and be sensible. An abortion's the only answer.

I can't! I won't!

It wasn't a matter of considering the fors-and-againsts of classroom discussion. Rationality had nothing to do with it. It was a primitive fear, a revulsion.

But the alternatives were even more frightening.

"Nine pounds a week," the man said. His name was Mr Pearson. He had a big square face and watery blue eyes that looked Abigail up and down as he spoke. "Rent in advance, and twenty pounds deposit."

"Deposit? What for?"

"In case of breakages or damage. You wouldn't get a furnished place without a deposit," Mr Pearson said.

He spoke as if he were offering penthouse

opulence. Abigail couldn't see anything that could be broken or damaged unless she deliberately smashed up the furniture. There wasn't much in the room at all: bed, formica-topped table with two upright chairs, wardrobe – well, *that* would be an improvement. Greyish carpet, faded flowered curtains. A tiny cooker and sink in one corner, with a small cupboard on the wall above. No pretensions to a sea view – the room looked over a garden that was more like a junk-yard. Abigail told herself that the room had everything she needed, and tried to imagine it brightened by posters on the wall, a colourful bedspread and a reading lamp.

"What about the bathroom?" she asked, trying to sound businesslike.

"Along the hall, shared with the flat above. Bathroom and WC separate." Mr Pearson hoisted himself up from his leaning position in the doorway and stumped along the narrow corridor.

Abigail followed. The whole place was bland and cheerless, but it was cleaner than 32 Princeton Terrace. She had already made up her mind. She wouldn't be disturbed here. There was a newsagent's underneath (handy, because it sold milk and bread) and another bedsit above: Holiday Flats, Mr Pearson called them. He'd probably want her out by next tourist season. But that was a long way off.

"Thanks," she said. "When can I move in?"

Saturday 19 October

I did something really stupid today. I thought it would be like in films, where the heroine's horse bolts and throws her and she has a miscarriage. It was a stupid thing to do.

It was a strange day. A mist, almost a fog, hung over the coast, hushing and deadening all sound. There were few people about and even the sea was subdued, the waves meeting the shingle with barely a ripple, as if the sea couldn't summon the energy for a proper high tide. Looking out from the promenade Abigail saw only whiteness, an indefinable haze which made her eyes swim.

She caught the ferry across the estuary and got out on the wooden jetty at the far side. There were only two other passengers and she supposed that the ferry, like almost everything else, would pack up for the winter soon; then the only way across the river would be by the road bridge two miles inland. She had crossed this way twice before, with Paul, to walk along the cliff path.

Last time, he had run ahead of her up the steep path and had mocked her for being slow. She could see him now, his teeth white in a tanned face, laughing at her in his teasing way.

Knowing that he hadn't really loved her did not lessen the acute wrench of loss. In spite of all his failings she sometimes found herself inventing excuses for him. He hadn't meant to go; he had gone further down the coast to find a nice flat for the two of them for the winter, and soon he'd come back to surprise her – Oh, don't be so *stupid*, she would scold herself when she came back to her senses. She despaired of herself, knowing that she would believe any lie of Paul's – *had* believed – because she wanted to. It was easier to tell herself that she hated him, but she didn't really want her present disillusionment to spread its taint backwards, polluting her whole view of him. She could think of him as two people: the charming, carefree lover and the faithless deserter. She could remember one and despise the other.

They had sat on the rounded summit looking across at the harbour. It was a sharp, clearly sunlit day; the sea danced with points of light and the air smelled warmly of grass and heather. By the cliff edge they had watched the white seabirds with their blobby black eyes and stiff wings planing the wind. "Fulmars," she had said, and Paul had said, "What, those birds? I thought they were just gulls. How do you know a thing like that?"

She knew because her parents had shown her fulmars and kittiwakes on boat trips around sea cliffs in Scotland. They had peered up with binoculars, Charlie endlessly patient until she had been able to identify the kittiwake with its darker chick balanced on a toehold of ledge, the fulmar riding the air on straight wings. It had been part of going on holiday with Mum and Dad: looking for birds, looking them up in books.

Now, slogging up the path, wondering if she was more breathless than usual and if it was because of the parasitic thing inside her, she felt a tug of hopeless regret, not for Paul this time but for childhood holidays when she had been cared for and looked after, with nothing more serious to worry about than tar on her shorts. Life could never be so simple again.

There were no fulmars today. No seabirds at all, as if this strange white mist held everything in suspension. The dampness on the short grass was dew, not rain, but it soaked through her plimsolls just as quickly. She reached the summit, venturing close to the edge and then a little closer. The waves below sent up a faint murmur, their sound rising through the mist to wash around inside her head, soothing and mesmerizing. Looking down gave no sense of perspective; the cliff edge fell into pearly haze. One step forward without thinking too much about it, and her problems would be over. A body washed up in the bay in a few days' time, perhaps, a short paragraph in the local paper. Finished.

But she was rejecting the idea even as it took shape in her mind. Before, Paul had laughed at her for her fear of heights, standing deliberately close to the edge to flaunt his recklessness, so close that a crumbling of the dry soil or a slip of the foot could throw him down to the rocks beneath. The fear she had felt then overcame her now, a physical fear that gripped her stomach muscles and clutched at her throat. Her feet were shuffling back from the edge, moving her to safety. Her body had its own instinct for survival, independent of her brain. She walked on disconsolately, knowing that she didn't have the courage for such a defiant gesture; she had never seriously intended it.

A new idea was taking shape, however. Beyond the summit, where the green slope swooped into a dip like a giant wave before rising again, there was a grassy path down to a cove. It wasn't so steep as to require actual climbing with handholds, but precipitous enough to need care when descending. Near the bottom it levelled out, reaching the sand and shingle of the secluded cove. Paul had run and slithered down with yodelling cries, and then sat on a rock skimming stones into the water and waiting for Abigail to edge her way down cautiously.

Today she would run. It wasn't like stepping off the edge of the summit, with only sheer rock punctuated by clumps of thrift and fulmars' ledges between her and the tide-swept rocks. Here it would be a calculated risk; she had seen how Paul teetered and skidded.

There was no one about. She took a deep breath and started to jog-trot down the path. She could see only a few yards ahead and then the enveloping mist, with some crags of rock looming eerily. Her feet slapped down on the path, an ankle twisting as the track veered unexpectedly. She couldn't stop now if she tried, her own momentum propelling her downwards. Too fast, as if something was pushing her, too fast for her eyes to pick out the next safe foothold, her feet flying blindly into space. And then both feet went skidding from under her; her arms flailed and one knee twisted painfully, and she was down, sprawling. She let herself roll, her face full of grass and sky and mist, her body thrown about like a rag doll, buffeted by the uneven ground, her breath jolted out of her.

Just as she had intended.

Her head was whirling so much that it took a few moments to realize that she wasn't rolling any more. She lay winded, her fingers clutching at a bristly tuft of grass, and then got slowly to her feet. Not used to strenuous exercise, she had underestimated the physical shock. She felt sick, shaken; her legs almost buckled under her as she stood. But this was why she had done it, to feel sick and shaken. She was not sure what she hoped for next; in films, the scene would simply cut to the grave-faced doctor coming out of the bedroom, breaking the news to the husband, the heroine wan and weeping in bed: "I'm so sorry, darling . . . our baby . . ." Except that it wasn't a baby yet, in her case, just a fragile collection of cells. Surely it couldn't have held on, through all that pummelling? Abigail felt steamrollered.

She was all alone on the small beach. She walked to the tide's edge and then waded in up to her shins. The water filling her plimsolls, tugging at her jeans, was a cold shock, numbing and then gradually thawing; the sea was slow to lose the summer's warmth. The strange atmosphere of the day reached her, calming her breathing to match the air's stillness. The mist was a physical presence, a bowl of opaque light holding sea, sky and cliffs in hushed isolation, as if nothing beyond existed. She could shout at the top of her voice and no one would hear; the mist would swallow and absorb any sound she made. The waves lifted and surged at her ankles, breaking gently on the stones and then sucking back with a rhythmic, hypnotic swish. Primeval soup, she thought, remembering science lessons; all life had come from the sea, single cells evolving into primitive creeping things that had dragged themselves ashore at the dawn of the world. Life would take a hold wherever it could, creatures living and dying, surviving and adapting, with a blind tenacity that defied human understanding.

Like the living thing inside her, determined to survive and be born. Her body was healthy, the doctor had said; a young, healthy body, perfectly designed for reproduction, and that was what it was going to do.

She waded ashore and took off her soaked plimsolls and sat on a rock, unaccountably calm. Her plan showed no sign of working but she knew that she had no further intention of interfering with the single-purposed determination of the life force inside her. She was going to have a baby.

After a while, too cold to sit any longer, she put her shoes on and made her way carefully up the cliff path, and went home to pack her belongings. Tomorrow she would move into Mr Pearson's bedsit.

Friday 25 October

My first week of living alone. I've done my first week at South Devon Insurers too, and it feels like half a century. It got deadlier and deadlier as the week went on. The whole place is stuck in a time warp – typists in twin sets, manual typewriters, dusty old cabinets, millions of smudgy carbon copies to be corrected by hand whenever you make a mistake. That's quite often, in my case. I'm the only person under thirty and it's so dull – everyone works without talking and in coffee breaks they gossip about their gardens and their holidays and their children. I try not to look at the clock too often because the time drags past so slowly. I keep thinking about the fifteen pounds at the end of the week to keep me going. Mrs Swain has worked there sixteen years – it'd drive me dotty. She calls me dear and talks to me as if I'm about fourteen. "Louise is the one who's – you know – expecting," she said, as if I'm too young to know what that means. She'll have a fit when she finds out I'm shh – you know – expecting, too. How long before it starts to show? I'm already planning for that, wearing my baggiest skirt with a big loose cardigan over it so that no one will notice the difference later.

Anyway, I've got my fifteen pounds and they told Mrs A B C I can come back next week, so I'm in, for what it's worth. I've got to register for National Insurance and open a bank account. I'm getting so organized!

Saturday 26 October

Went to the supermarket and the launderette and then the library.

Abigail lay in bed, relishing the prospect of two days away from South Devon Insurers. Saturday morning – her first weekend in her own bedsit. Her own home, such as it was! She could get up when she chose, and make breakfast without having to do a week's washing-up first. She had not considered what to do after going to the supermarket and launderette; she was content to lie in bed and doze, too lazy to stretch out a hand to turn on the radio. The room didn't look quite so bad now that she was getting used to it. She had stuck up *Les Coquelicots* and various postcards to make it look more cheerful. Early in the morning a shaft of sunlight reached in to light one corner of the room, the only time of day this was possible since the room faced east, but it made it pleasant to lie in bed.

She could get up, but it would be cold – the electric heater was expensive and took a while to take effect. There was no hurry. She yawned and stretched, listening to voices from the newsagent's downstairs. Its door jangled each time it was opened or closed, which happened from seven-thirty onwards, but that was the only disturbance and it made a useful alarm clock for weekdays.

She looked up at the dingy ceiling. It was odd to think that while she was lying here, doing nothing, her body was industriously working away at all its functions; her lungs were processing air, heart pumping away, hair and nails growing, cells renewing themselves. And another person was growing inside her. She had looked in the pregnancy book from the library and knew that at eight weeks it wasn't yet recognizably a baby, more like a funny-shaped tadpole; but it already had a miniscule heart beating and it contained all the ingredients to become a human being, a person. It was a miracle, when she thought of it like that.

It wasn't always going to seem miraculous, she knew. Before long she would have to sort out a lot of things. What was she going to live on, for a start, when the baby came? How was she going to look after it? She didn't know the first thing about babies. But all that could wait. For now, it was Saturday morning and the sun was shining, and everything was all right. She rolled over and closed her eyes.

Later, lingering unnecessarily in the supermarket to look at things she didn't want and couldn't afford, it occurred to her for the first time that a whole weekend was a very long time to spend by herself. She had escaped from everyone she didn't want to see, but now she was completely alone, without a single friend for company. She had achieved her independence a little too successfully. What was she going to do? It was only lunchtime and the day had turned grey and blustery, discouraging hanging about outside. If only Claudia hadn't gone back to Berlin they could have gone to the pub together, or to the cinema.

Then she thought of the library. It wasn't as big or as well-stocked as the one at home but still she could spend some time there. Inside, she went to the journals section to look for the local paper. A few old men in drab macs or jackets sat at the tables, each in isolation, elbows spread over the open pages of newspapers. Lonely people, like me, she thought; whiling away the hours, gathering in a warm place where they can sit undisturbed. Where do they go when the library closes? Despondency overwhelmed her, defeating the optimism of the morning. Look at me, she thought hopelessly: lumbered with a deadly job that will have me screaming with boredom in a fortnight, and a one-room flat that I don't want to go back to, and no friends. No one knows where I am and no one cares. I'm eighteen, she thought bitterly: I should be having *fun*. Saturdays were for parties, for going out with friends, for spending ages getting ready, for eyeing the boys and laughing hysterically at nothing at all. That part of her life seemed years ago. But I chose this, she thought. I was fed up with home; I wanted this instead. She tried to remember all the rows with her parents, but found herself thinking that she might have passed her driving test by now if she had stayed at home, and that Charlie had mentioned getting her a little second-hand car for her eighteenth birthday. She had chosen this; she had chosen freedom. Freedom! She could have laughed out loud. Freedom to wander round a public library on Saturday for want of anywhere else to go? Freedom to choose one tin of backed beans rather than another? So much for her dreams of long hot summer days, of the happy commune of artists, of the creativity which would flourish once the bonds of convention were thrown off . . .

She could not cope with her see-sawing feelings. Unable to face going out to the drab street again and feeling her feet come to a standstill because she had no idea where to go next, she went over to the Art shelves and picked out a book at random. *Expressionism*. A picture flashed into her mind of Paul in the library at home, and she shoved the book back hastily and searched for another. *Seurat*. She had an idea that she liked Seurat. She opened the book and found herself looking at crayon drawings instead of the pointillist paintings she expected. Wonderful figure drawing, with depth and solidity, grace of line and curve. Taking the book to a table she sat and pored over the illustrations. How must it feel to draw like that? She thought of her own attempts, now shoved into a cupboard, and remembered the satisfaction of conjuring line and texture from the blank page, the excitement of seeing a picture emerge from her fingers, like a photograph developing.

She would go back to her drawing.

Part Five

Oddly enough, I can remember feeling highly pleased with myself for the first couple of days after I moved into my own bedsit and started work at the office. It was all so dreary, but I was independent, more so than I'd ever been in my life before. It was like playing at being grown-up. It was as if I'd proved to all of them – my parents, Jess, Paul – that I was managing on my own, that I hadn't given in. Leaving Princeton Terrace was another escape, smuggling my things out without anyone seeing, leaving a note and the money to pay my rent up to date. I'm not sure why I didn't simply tell them I was moving out; an urge for the dramatic gesture, perhaps, or else running away had become a habit. I suppose it seems odd now that I stayed at Chilcombe Sands. There was no reason to; I could have gone anywhere. That was partly why I *did* stay. When you realize you can go anywhere at all, and it doesn't make much difference where, the thought of casting yourself off from everything familiar is rather frightening. I wasn't brave enough.

I didn't even think of going home. It was the last thing I would have considered. It would have meant admitting that I couldn't cope. I couldn't bear the idea of telling them I was pregnant. Of course it was different then; to be an unmarried mother was to bring disgrace to your family. We'd had the permissive sixties, and attitudes do change, but they change slowly. I was soon to find that out.

But I *thought* about home – wondering what they were all doing, whether they talked about me, or if they'd simply written me off as a bad lot. And, to be honest, I thought about the comforts of home that I'd always taken for granted: washing done, clothes ironed, a hot meal on the table every night. I'd have given a lot to have all that luxury again. But not by admitting defeat and going home. I preferred to shiver in my bedsit. It was so cold, once winter came! I used to sit as close to the electric heater as I could get, wearing thick tights and three jumpers. I used to listen to the radio all the time for company. I should have had an exhaustive knowledge of current affairs, the number of times I heard the radio news each day. There were the Watergate resignations, the Birmingham pub bomb, something nasty brewing up in Cambodia . . . I heard it all but I couldn't have explained what was going on. I was too concerned with myself to take any notice of the world at large. Those winter evenings . . . it must have been the loneliest time of my life. For weeks on end I spoke to no one between leaving the office and going back there next morning.

It was the drawing that kept me going. I've still got all my old sketchbooks. I couldn't afford paint so I used pencil or crayon, copying from books or working up my sketches from the summer. Sometimes when it was mild at the weekend I'd go down to the harbour or the beach. And I really did begin to improve. It takes a while to develop a style of your own and to stop copying other people.

I must have known that I wouldn't be able to carry on like that for ever. Making up my mind about the baby made me feel calm, in a strange way. I'd made a choice, not because I was forced into it, but because I wanted the baby – wanted you. I knew there would be problems; sometimes I panicked, but not enough to make me think seriously about what would happen once you came. I pushed that to the back of my mind. I was good at ignoring things.

* * * *

Thursday 19 December
Bumped into Gillian in the supermarket.

Almost five-thirty. Mrs Swain was already into her going-home ritual, peering into a small mirror to tweak at her stiffly-permed hair and powder her face. Abigail was typing furiously, glancing at the clock. She thought she had finished today's letters until Mrs Swain had pointed out two spelling mistakes.

"They're typing mistakes, not spelling mistakes," Abigail retorted, but the difference was unimportant to Mrs Swain, who said, "You'll have time to do it again, if you hurry."

Abigail was holding her breath in case she made another mistake. *Yours faithfully, P. Maltravers, Claims Manager, South Devon Insurers*. There: finished. She separated the letter from its carbon copies and slapped it with its envelope on Mrs Swain's desk.

"Bye then, all," Mr Maltravers called cheerily, emerging from his inner sanctum on the stroke of five-thirty, as usual. It was the cue for everyone else to get to their feet, shrugging into coats and picking up shopping bags.

"I'll sign this for him, to save leaving it till the morning," Mrs Swain said. She made Abigail wait while she read the letter very carefully before signing it. "I wish you'd remember to centre *Yours faithfully*, dear."

"We didn't learn it that way at college. We were taught to do everything against the margin. It's more modern."

"It's up to Mr Maltravers to decide how he likes his letters set out, don't you think?" Mrs Swain said, although Abigail was certain that Mr Maltravers couldn't care less, since he gave the letters no more than a cursory glance before signing them with great loops and flourishes, in flamboyant contrast to the dry contents. "Do remember in future. You haven't forgotten the post, have you?"

"No, of course not," Abigail said. She folded the offending letter into its envelope and sealed and stamped it. Mrs Swain was ostentatiously checking round the office, waiting for Abigail to go so that she could lock up. Abigail threw the cover over her typewriter and groped underneath it for the disc-shaped rubber that she was always losing. Her fingers smelled of carbon paper and rubber dust, dead office smells. She put on the duffel coat, several sizes too large and helpfully concealing, which she had recently bought at a jumble sale. Her back ached and she wondered whether it was the long hours at the typist's chair that had caused it, or her pregnancy. It couldn't be long now before her expectant state became clear to everyone – she felt as if it were blazingly obvious now, but either the baggy clothes she always wore or a natural lack of observation had prevented Mrs Swain and the others from noticing. Perhaps they only thought she was a bit overweight.

She put on her gloves, picked up the bundle of letters and went out into the street. It was dark already, and an east wind made her fasten the top toggle of her duffel coat. Coloured lights were strung across the street and the shop windows were bright with Christmas trees and tinsel garlands. Christmas! What was she going to do over the Christmas break? Sit on her own and listen to carols on the radio? She usually enjoyed all the preparations: making lists, buying and wrapping presents and hiding them in her room, decorating the tree. This year she had no one to buy a present for. Christmas would be a few blank days to get through, an intensification of her loneliness – a mockery of the independence she had sought so diligently. She would have to hibernate.

She posted the letters and went to the Co-op to buy something for her tea. Cheese on toast or baked beans were the most she usually aspired to, with coffee and biscuits for later. She put a sliced loaf into her basket and was moving towards the jam shelves when her eye was caught by a familiar figure – Gillian, walking slowly towards her, reading a shopping list. Gillian looked up as she drew level, her eyes widening in surprise.

"Abigail! What are you doing here?"

"Getting some shopping."

"No, I mean you're still living down here? Jess said you'd gone back home after . . . after Paul left. I'd no idea you were still around."

"I didn't tell her where I was going," Abigail said, somewhat embarrassed. She should have said goodbye to Gillian, at least. "I left the money and cleared off."

"But where to? Where are you living?"

"In a little flat – bedsit, really – up past the cinema." Abigail felt ashamed of her exile, remembering Gillian's bright well-ordered room. Gillian seemed to carry an air of exoticism with her, even standing in the supermarket by the peeled plum tomatoes. She wore a long hooded cloak and her turquoise ikat scarf, and made everyone else look drab. Abigail felt a sudden rush of warmth towards her, because she was the nearest thing to a friend.

Gillian's dark eyes regarded Abigail seriously. "Are you managing on your own?"

"Yes, just about. I've got a job – a deadly one, but still a job."

Gillian looked at her watch. "I'm going home after this – why don't you come with me and have something to eat? Or are you doing something else?"

"No, nothing else. Thanks, but—"

"What's the problem?"

Abigail hesitated. "Well, I'd like to come, but I'm not sure about meeting Jess and Bill. Not after doing a moonlight flit."

"You needn't worry." They had started to walk slowly down the aisle and Gillian took a wholemeal loaf from the shelves. "They're not at home tonight. They've gone to Bristol to see someone Bill knows about fittings for the gallery. There's just me and Beano, and Max – oh, you don't know Max, do you? He's a student from Exeter. But he probably won't be in either."

"Thanks, then. I will," Abigail said gratefully.

It felt strange to go in at the door of 32 Princeton Terrace. The 2 was still hanging loose, the familiar smell of greasy cooking hung in the air and heavy rock thumped down from Beano's room. Banishing the thought that the front bedroom door might open and that Paul might come out, grinning casually and asking where she'd been all this time – Oh, don't be *stupid*! – Abigail followed Gillian to the top floor and through the door with the beadwork hanging. Gillian flicked the light on and Abigail stood in the doorway registering an unfamiliar sensation.

"It's *warm* in here!"

"Yes, but only after a battle." Gillian flung her cloak on the bed, unwound her scarf and filled the kettle from a jug. "I had to get Bill's uncle round and make him get the central heating sorted out. It was ridiculous for all of us to be huddling round separate electric heaters. They're expensive to run, and there was a perfectly good central heating system that only needed servicing and a valve replaced. And there was no hot water, which was worse."

She had switched on an Art Deco lamp, which made the room look warm and welcoming: a home, not a temporary refuge like Abigail's. Impressed, Abigail took off her duffel coat and reached up to hang it behind the door. It was an unguarded movement and she looked round to see Gillian staring at her in transparent dismay.

"*Abby!* You're – you're – I didn't *realize*—"

Abigail hunched her cardigan round her shoulders defensively, but it was too late. "Oh, God, does it show? Yes, I am. I'm pregnant."

Gillian was crouching on the floor, kettle in hand, shocked into stillness. "But when—? How long have you known? Did Paul know?"

"Yes, he did," Abigail said flatly. "That was the main reason why he left in such a hurry."

"Oh, *Abby*—" Gillian stood up and ushered Abigail towards the bed and made her sit down. "You must be in a terrible state, all on your own – is that why you left here? You didn't want anyone to know?"

Abigail nodded, afraid that she would cry if she tried to explain. She thought she had done all the crying she was ever going to do, but tears still sprang readily. She wasn't used to sympathy, having cultivated an image of bright self-sufficient nonchalance which she presented to the outside world. Her fortifications were in danger of crumbling, faced with Gillian's concern.

"I'm glad you know now, anyway," she said.

Gillian sat down beside her. "And Paul cleared off and left you to cope? The *bastard*."

She said it so fiercely that Abigail suddenly found herself giggling instead of crying. The harsh word sounded so odd, coming from Gillian. "Yes, he is," she said weakly. "But it was my fault too. I was an idiot."

"What are you going to do? You can't stay on your own."

"Yes, I can. I'll have to."

"But when the baby's born? Do your parents know?"

"God, no. They're the last people I'd think of telling. They'd kill me. No one knows. Only you and the doctor. And Paul."

Gillian looked doubtful. "When's the baby due? Are you sure it wouldn't be better to go home to your parents?" She put up a hand to cut off Abigail's objection. "Of course it would be a shock for them, it would be for most parents. But they'd get over it, wouldn't they? I'm sure they'd want you to be looked after properly, not try to survive on a shoe-string."

"Well, who doesn't?" Abigail said. "No one here's ever got any money."

"But we're not all in your situation. Are you really planning to keep the baby?"

"Oh yes." Abigail's protective instincts rose quickly. "I didn't want an abortion. I've chosen not to have one. The baby will be due about June."

"Abortion isn't the only possibility. I meant are you going to put it up for adoption?"

"Can you do that? Hand it over to someone else?" Abigail hadn't thought of that. Now that she was going to have the baby, she intended to keep it – not *it*, but a baby son or daughter. She briefly considered the escape offered by Gillian's suggestion. She could have her teenage life back. She could be a normal eighteen-year-old with only herself to consider.

"Of course you can," Gillian said. "There are hundreds of couples who want babies but can't have them, you must know that. The baby's taken away from you as soon as it's born, if it's going to be adopted – so that you don't get attached to it and then change your mind."

"No, I'm not giving it up," Abigail said. "I'm going to keep it. I don't know how, but I am. I'm so ignorant. I don't know how to go on the dole or get maternity allowances or anything. And I certainly don't know how to have a baby." She leaned against the batik cushions, suddenly light-headed, as if nothing mattered very much. Her secret, so carefully-guarded up till now, was out in the open, already accepted by Gillian. She was enormously relieved. People had babies all the time, after all; it wasn't anything out of the ordinary. It was a natural thing to do.

"It's easy enough to find out about the allowances and so forth. I'll help you, if you like." Gillian got up to make the coffee. "Did you say you had a job?"

"Yes. A mind-blowingly dull one, but still a job. Typing and filing, and then home to my room, that's my life at the moment. It's so nice to be away from there for an evening. I'm beginning to feel like a hermit."

"You should have kept in touch," Gillian said. "I'm always here on my own."

"Yes, I should," Abigail said feelingly. She noticed several rectangular objects wrapped in black plastic and propped against the wall. "Have you been doing a lot of painting? Is it still going well?"

"Quite well. I'll tell you about it in a

minute," Gillian said. "I'll get us something to eat, but first you're going to have to make a promise."

Abigail looked up suspiciously, expecting an attempt to persuade her to go home. "What?"

"That you're going to look after yourself better," Gillian said.

Friday 20 December

It was great to see Gillian yesterday. She was so nice, and it made such a change to have someone to talk to. She's invited me to an exhibition of her paintings in Exeter tomorrow night, a special preview evening. I'm looking forward to it.

Saturday 21 December

Went to Gillian's exhibition. It was really impressive. Met Max.

"Max will give you a lift," Gillian had said. "I'll be going over first thing in the morning to set things up, and then I'm going back to Henry's house – he's the gallery owner – to change before the evening do."

Abigail wasn't sure about driving to Exeter with the unknown Max. She would have preferred to go by herself on the train, rather than make polite conversation with a stranger; but it would have seemed ridiculous to refuse, and Gillian would be coming back in the car with them afterwards.

For some reason the name Max had made her picture a burly blond six-footer. Meeting her at the pre-arranged spot outside Boots, Max turned out to be slim and dark, dressed in jeans and an Afghan coat and a bead necklace: not at all the rugby-playing type she had imagined. It had occurred to her that maybe Bill and Jess were going to the exhibition – surely they would be looking on Gillian as a future protégée for their own gallery? She asked Max, but he said no, they weren't coming.

"I don't think their plans are working out too well, to be honest. The last I heard, they were talking of turning it into a craft and souvenir shop."

"What, seaside souvenirs? Postcards and stuff?"

"I suppose they've got a point," Max said. "They've got to make ends meet. It's hard to see how a new place starting from scratch would be able to compete with established galleries like the one we're going to."

Abigail saw what he meant as soon as they entered the Cathedral Gallery. Although not extensive – it consisted of small rooms opening off a reception area where drinks were being served – it was discreetly elegant, with soft lighting and paintings individually spotlit. A single oil landscape stood on an easel in the front window, where Gillian's name was displayed with those of the three other artists whose work was exhibited. It was a setting completely unfamiliar to Abigail, who hadn't had an evening out for months, let alone at a place like this where people dressed with expensive casualness and contemplated buying pictures for hundreds of pounds. She couldn't even see Gillian and was glad now that she had come with Max; she would have felt out of place on her own. Perhaps Gillian had thought of that.

The gallery owner, a man of about fifty with a bow tie and a tweed jacket and long backswept grey hair, came to greet them. "Friends of Gillian? So glad you could come. Do come through – wine, white or red?"

Abigail wasn't at all sure that she ought to be drinking alcohol, especially after the lecture Gillian had given her about the importance of a healthy diet. She looked doubtfully at the glass of wine Henry had pressed on her and wondered whether Max knew she was pregnant. Would Gillian have mentioned it, Abigail wondered? She was wearing the dark green tunic, the one Paul had liked, although at present it was concealed beneath her duffel coat, which made her feel extremely shabby against the surrounding sleekness.

"There she is," Max said. Gillian was surrounded by people, but she saw them and waved and then detached herself to come over and say hello. Before she reached them, Henry intercepted to introduce some new arrivals: "Mr and Mrs Smythe – they're so interested in your work," and Gillian was led away again towards the room where her paintings were displayed. She was wearing a dress of rich dark red with a black and red scarf and long silver earrings; Abigail thought she looked marvellous.

Max smiled ruefully. "We're not going to get a look in. She's obviously in great demand. Let's look at the paintings."

The room was full of pictures in Gillian's distinctive style and vibrant colours. Her subjects were simple: a fish, a bird in a tree, a cat, painted in what appeared as glowing fragments of light, with an effect like stained glass. The roomful was dazzling. Abigail noticed that several pictures had red stickers on the labels to show that they were sold. She was deeply impressed by Gillian's determination as much as by her success – the confidence she must have, to know what she wanted to do and to work hard at it, alone and without recognition for most of the time. Glittering occasions like this were rare, the hard-earned reward for months of solitary work. Gillian never made a fuss about it, or complained, or drew attention to herself; she just got on with it. She had no trace of what Abigail had once thought of as an artistic temperament, but perhaps a true artistic temperament was shown more in the ability to sit down and work than in showy flashes. Of all of them in the house, for all the airy plans that had been talked of at first, Gillian was the only one who actually did anything. Unless Max . . . ? He had mentioned in the car that he was training to be an art teacher, and had told her some funny stories about his disastrous first teaching practice.

"What sort of things do you paint?" she asked him.

"Nothing to compare with this. I draw a bit, but I haven't got Gillian's self-discipline. What about you?"

"Me? No, nothing like this. I mean, I'd like to paint but I'm no good. I'm trying to learn to draw."

Max looked interested. "Do you go to a class?"

"No. I started going to a life class at home but then I—" She hesitated, wondering whether Gillian had told him about Paul. "Then I came down here and I haven't been since. I practise by myself though and work from books."

"The WEA does a good life class," Max said. "I go along most weeks. It's at the secondary school by the bridge. The classes have stopped now for the holidays, but they start up again in the New Year."

"The WEA?"

"Workers' Educational Association," Max said. "The tutor's very good. You might find it helpful. The classes are on Thursdays. I could easily give you a lift if you wanted to go."

"Thanks. I'd like to."

It had been too dark in the car for her to receive more than a dim impression of Max's appearance. Now, looking at him properly, it occurred to her that he lived in the room she had shared with Paul; he slept in their bed. She wondered whether he always slept there alone. He had an unusual face, too sharp and bony to be good-looking, but with brown eyes expressing warmth and intelligence. A very drawable face, she thought, her fingers itching for a pencil. She wasn't sure whether he was showing interest in her by suggesting the life class, or simply being friendly. She found herself hoping for the former. *Stop* it, she reprimanded herself; you can't start thinking like that, not now! She wondered what Max would say if she remarked, "I'm having a baby in June." He would probably be concerned, like Gillian, and fetch her a chair to sit on; he was kind, she could tell. And she felt an ache of loneliness, because the game of making herself look attractive and fancying people and chatting-up, and all that went with it, was one she could no longer play; not now, not for a long time. She had put herself on the sidelines. Who would ever want her?

It was a short distance from here to total panic, she knew. She sometimes terrified herself in the middle of the night with thoughts of something going wrong, a miscarriage or some other disaster, while she was all alone with no one to call for help. She tried to think about something else. What had they been talking about just now? Oh yes, the life class. She remembered sitting at an easel next to Paul when he was still a glamorous newcomer to her life. Would she ever be able to trust anyone again? She looked at Max's gaunt, expressive face, aware of a definite flicker of attraction in spite of her doubts. There was nothing about him to suggest arrogance or self-regard.

"Shall we look at one of the other rooms?" she suggested, dismayed by the way her thoughts were running.

"Yes. Would you like some more wine?"

Her glass was empty, in spite of her doubts about drinking. They made their way through to the reception room, where Gillian pushed her way through the chattering groups towards them.

"Hello! Are you all right? Sorry I've abandoned you!"

Max put an arm round her. "Here's the star

of the show. Don't worry, we're fine. How's it going?"

"Well, I think. Have you looked at Ivan's screen prints yet? They're brilliant."

Monday 23 December

An awful day.

Mrs Swain knows. I wonder how *long* she's known, and all the time I've been kidding myself. They've probably been talking about me when I'm not there. I hate the thought of that.

She asked me to stay behind after work and she came straight out with it – "When's the baby due, dear?" I must have stood with my mouth open like a fish. She said I should have told them when they took me on, even though I'm only a temp. Then she started nosing around and trying to find out whether my parents know, and where my boyfriend is and whether I'm going to get married. I should have told her to mind her own business but instead I acted superior and offended. She said, "I'm only trying to help, dear."

I hope she won't get me kicked out. They only have to tell Mrs A B C they don't want me next week, and that's my lot. I'd be lucky to get anything else in the middle of winter.

I don't want to find out about the dole, not yet.

Gillian came round. I showed her my drawings and she liked them. I'm really jealous of her – I know I shouldn't be but I can't help it. She's always so nice to me and I shouldn't grudge her anything, and that makes me feel even worse. But I can't stop myself from envying her, especially now. She's got everything I wish I had.

Abigail, expecting Mr Pearson for the rent, went to answer a knock at the door and found Gillian standing there.

"Hello! I said I'd come to see where you live. Are you busy?"

"No – come in."

Abigail had been huddling over the electric heater, working at a drawing: copying and working up a quick sketch of people in the High Street. She closed the sketchbook hastily and straightened the bedspread. She knew how drab and uninspired the room must look to Gillian, used to her own colourful haven. Abigail's attempts at brightening it up – the Monet poppies, some postcards and a couple of her own sketches – merely emphasized the dull functionality of everything else. There were two Christmas cards stuck on the wall with Blu-Tak: one from Gillian and one from South Devon Insurers, with a standard greeting printed inside.

"I'll make some tea." She turned the electric heater to face the bed so that Gillian wouldn't freeze while she waited. Gillian wisely didn't remove her cloak; she sat on the bed, not speaking, while Abigail filled the kettle, lit the gas ring and took a packet of biscuits out of the cupboard. Abigail saw Gillian noticing the contents of the food shelves, no doubt disapproving of the quantity of tins and packets inside, the complete lack of fruit and vegetables. Abigail had tried making a casserole once and the room reeked of fried onions for days afterwards, getting into her hair and her clothes. Baked beans were easier.

"Let me see the drawings!" Gillian said, seeing the sketchbook.

"There's nothing interesting in it," Abigail said quickly. "Only some rough sketches."

Gillian paused, one hand extended. "But can I?"

"If you really want to."

Abigail busied herself with making the tea, not wanting to see Gillian's reactions. She recognized the feebleness of her efforts compared to Gillian's, no matter how hard she laboured. Max had probably seen better results in his classroom on teaching practice, any day of the week.

"Here," she said, embarrassed, passing Gillian a mug of tea.

Gillian looked up. "These are really good, Abby. You've made such an improvement . . ." She leafed back to the beginning of the book.

"These are far better than the ones you showed me at first."

"Really? You're not just saying that?"

"No!" Gillian said sharply. "I wouldn't say it unless I really thought so. Look at this, and this . . . the strength of line, the pose of that figure . . . Lots of people at art school can't draw as well as this."

"Oh, you're joking!"

"I'm *not* joking," Gillian insisted. "What have you been doing, shut away up here all this time?"

"Only looking at books, and wandering about with a sketchbook. Nothing much."

Gillian smiled. "You don't have to sound furtive about it. It's your work. It's what you do. It's important, if you want it to be."

"I suppose you're right." Abigail tried out Gillian's way of thinking and found it pleasant. *My work*. It made her sound like a proper artist. All the effort was worth it, if Gillian was right. She wasn't deluding herself; she was achieving something. In the New Year she would go to the life class with Max, and get some real tuition . . .

"Did you like Max?" Gillian asked casually, as if picking up the thought.

"Oh – yes," Abigail said. "Yes, I did."

Gillian sipped her tea and then glanced at her, looking almost furtive herself.

"I came partly to tell you," she said, "that I'm going away for a few days, over Christmas and after. I know you'll be here on your own – I would have asked you to come, if I could. But . . . well, I'm . . . I mean we're . . . going to my parents, and then I'm going to stay with Max for a couple of days. His family lives in Somerset."

Abigail was about to say, "What for?" when she noticed that Gillian was blushing.

"It's too early to tell how it'll work out with Max," Gillian said, fiddling with a frayed edge of the bedspread, "but so far . . . Oh, Abby, I never thought I'd find anyone so . . . well, so right! Someone who understands me, who's around but doesn't expect me to drop everything for him. And it was so odd, when we met – as soon as we looked at each other, it was as if we both *knew*. And he's so lovely, and funny, and thoughtful . . ." She sat forward clasping her knees, eager. "I've always got tired of people before. Nothing's ever lasted, with me – no one's been that important, I suppose. But it's different with Max . . . Oh, I'm sorry, Abby, going on like this! It's so new, and exciting – I can't stop talking about him."

"No, it's all right," Abigail said, conscious of how ungracious she sounded. She ought to be pleased, for goodness' sake! Instead, Gillian's words were like a door slamming in her face.

Max and Gillian loved each other. Of course they did. How had she failed to see it for herself on Saturday night? *Because I was stupid enough to think that Max might be interested in me*. She felt suddenly weary, in sharp contrast to Gillian's girlish excitement.

"Well, you're lucky," she said. "I hope it works out for you."

She wished she could find the generosity to sound more enthusiastic. It would work out, of course. Things did work out for Gillian. Gillian was attractive, and kind, and talented. And unencumbered.

Boxing Day

It's been an awful Christmas, not like Christmas at all. I'll be glad when it's all over. At least most of the time I can pretend to be normal, but not at Christmas when you're a misfit if you're not pulling crackers round the dinner table and wearing a paper hat. I've never known the time go so slowly. I've had the radio on all the time, but the programmes are so never-endingly jolly that I feel like throwing it out of the window.

I keep thinking of this time last year, Christmas at home. And not just last year but all the years before it. Granny Alice coming round, and all of us playing that silly game where we make hats out of wrapping paper and vote for the best one. Dad's idea. He was always good at silly games. Perhaps they're making hats now. I always imagine them thinking of me as dead. Do they talk about me? If they don't believe in me any more perhaps I'll disappear, like Tinkerbell.

Usually it's me pretending that *they* don't exist. Not letting myself think about them. It's as if I'm taking out a secret file and looking back through the pages. My past. I've put the secret locks on it but today I can't help taking them off for a sneaky look.

God, I'm writing a load of rubbish. It's the loneliness, rotting my brain.

Anyway, there's no doubt that I'm real – larger than life. It's amazing what difference two weeks makes. A fortnight ago I thought I could still hide the bulge in baggy clothes, but now it's quite obvious to anyone with eyes. Mr Pearson grinned at me in a funny way when he came round for the rent – I thought he was going to say something, but he didn't, though I'm sure he knows. People look at me in the street and in shops, and sometimes I can see them looking at my left hand to see if I'm wearing a ring. Unmarried mother, you can see them thinking, as if there are thought balloons above their heads. Got herself into trouble. Perhaps if I looked older they wouldn't do it so obviously.

I've even thought about buying myself a cheap wedding ring, but so far I've resisted it. Pretending to be married would be admitting defeat.

I'll be enormous soon. Sometimes I feel so frightened at the thought of losing control of my body. I can't stop myself, I can't do anything except grow. It's taking me over. And then at other times I feel quite content – proud, even, because I'm doing this all by myself. It was odd the other day when Mrs Swain asked me where my boyfriend was. For a minute I couldn't think who she was talking about. I haven't got a boyfriend. I don't think of this as Paul's baby – I've almost forgotten that he had anything to do with it. It's mine.

I thought about him after Gillian had gone, though. She was so full of excitement that it made me feel cautious and cynical, as if I was suddenly older than her. Don't get too carried away, I felt like saying – it might seem wonderful now but it might not always be like that. But who am I to talk, on the basis of my one relationship of just a few weeks? I could have had other chances, but I won't now. I might as well be middle-aged. I've had my chance and blown it. It seems so long ago now, that time when I thought Paul was everything I could dream of. He was never what I wanted him to be, but that was my fault, not his.

New Year's Eve

I've got to leave here. Soon. I don't feel safe here any more. I feel as if I'm being watched all the time. I feel dirty.

Abigail had been washing her underwear in the sink while she listened to a play on the radio. The washing was draped over a line she had strung from the top of the cupboard to one of the window latches, and she had made herself some cocoa, thinking that she might as well have an early night. Some New Year's Eve, she thought, with a mug of cocoa for celebration. Tomorrow it will be 1975, and the baby will be born *this year*: a few months away, countable in terms of weeks, days. Nine months had seemed to stretch into infinity at first but already the time span was shrinking, the end in sight. Except that it wasn't an end but a beginning. This time next year she'd be looking after a baby son or daughter of seven months . . .

The slow plod of footsteps up the stairs from the street door jerked her back to the present. Visitors were rare, if not unheard of; it couldn't be Gillian, since she was still away with Max, and in any case Gillian wouldn't clomp up heavily like that. It could only be Mr Pearson, but it seemed a very strange time for him to call. She had paid her rent up to date. Perhaps he had managed to let the upstairs flat at last, and someone was moving in . . .

The footsteps came along the corridor and halted outside, and there was an abrupt thump on the door.

Warily, Abigail opened it. Mr Pearson stood there, one hand resting on the door frame, his face flushed. She stared at him uncertainly.

"Aren't you going to let me in?" he said, grinning.

Usually he stood outside in the hallway with his rent book while she handed him her money, not stopping for conversation. She was not sure that she wanted conversation now, but she could hardly refuse to let him come in, it being his flat. She caught the smell of whisky on his breath as he passed. He wore a navy-blue anorak, and his thin dark hair was slicked greasily across the flat top of his head.

"All on your own tonight, then?" he said, as if it weren't obvious. "I saw your light on."

"Yes."

"What, no parties to go to? No boyfriend to keep you company? A pretty girl like you?"

She didn't like the way he was looking at her – appraising and scornful at the same time – nor the way he was standing a little too close. She moved back into the room and stood behind a wooden chair, resting her hands on the back. "Did you want something?" she asked coolly.

"Not going to be on your own for much longer, are you?" he said, not answering. His eyes moved down her body and up again and he smiled at her unpleasantly.

She looked straight back at him. "No. I'm going to have a baby."

"Oh dear, oh dear." He made a tutting sound with his tongue and shook his head reprovingly. "Got yourself into trouble, have you?"

"What have you come to say?" Abigail said. Her voice was not quite steady.

"It's time we sorted a few things out." Mr Pearson misunderstood her gesture with the chair, thinking she was inviting him to sit down. He held out a hand towards the bed, indicating that she should sit down too, but she chose to remain standing. She wanted him to say what he wanted to say, quickly, and then go. Sitting on the bed would be too suggestive of friendly intimacy.

"What do you want to sort out?" she said, trying to sound calm and aloof.

"The point is," Mr Pearson said, "you weren't straight with me when you first came here, were you? I agreed to let the flat to you but that's not to say you can bring a baby here. Single occupancy, these flats are."

"Oh yes? When there's a double bed?"

The thrust of Mr Pearson's jaw showed his dislike of being challenged. "For holiday lets, those double beds are. Winter arrangements is different. Single occupancy. If you'd've told me you was expecting, when you first came here, I wouldn't have been as quick to say yes."

"So what are you saying? That I've got to move out?"

Her directness took him off guard. She could see his mind working, his eyes shifting behind drawn-down brows.

"Nothing as hasty as that, like. Not straight away. What I'm getting at is, come the summer, I can charge for a family room. Whereas if you stayed on at the rate I'm charging now, you'd be getting double occupancy for the price of one."

"When I have the baby, you're going to charge me double rent?"

"If you want to put it like that, yes. That's if I agree to have the baby here at all. Babies, toddlers, they're a bit of a problem, you see. We might end up with all sorts of damage."

He looked around the room as if it were five-star accommodation. Abigail could hardly refrain from laughing, for all her despondency at what he was saying. "Don't your holiday people ever bring babies with them?" she asked.

"There's not room, is there? A baby in a cot, maybe."

"So then you'd charge them triple, if there were two people and a baby?"

Mr Pearson leaned forward. "Look. What I charge for my holiday lets is up to me. I'm just telling you straight. We'll have to see how it goes with the baby, and you're going to have to pay double rent if you want to stay. Same as anyone else would pay if they rented it for a holiday."

Abigail was silent for a moment, thinking. Was he entitled to put the rent up, just as he chose? She didn't have anything in writing. She had no idea what her entitlement was. Gillian would know; she would have to ask Gillian. Mr Pearson, obviously feeling that his point had sunk in at last, sat back in his chair and gazed with interest at the knickers and tights hanging on the washing line. Abigail felt as if she were undressing in front of him.

"I'll go somewhere else," she said sharply. "Don't worry. Yours aren't the only holiday flats available. I wouldn't want you to worry about your precious furnishings."

What was she saying? Where else could she go? This room, basic and unwelcoming as it was, had become her *home*, her territory.

Mr Pearson's watery, almost colourless eyes dragged themselves away from the underwear and swivelled back to rest on Abigail's face.

"Now, now, there's no need to take that attitude," he said, his voice wheedling. "You don't have to do anything hasty."

He bared his teeth in a grin and stood up. Abigail moved towards the door, thinking he was going at last. He intercepted her, placing a hand on her arm. She looked at him in surprise. His face was sweaty, in spite of the chill of the room, and his mouth hung open, half-smiling.

"We could sort something out, you and me . . . Your boyfriend cleared off, did he? You're missing him, aren't you? Been a silly girl, haven't you?"

Abigail backed away hastily but he lunged towards her, swaying slightly. Before she could dodge away he had her pinned against the wall, his body pressing against hers, one knee pushing between her legs. She could smell whisky, and the stale sweat and cigarette smoke on his clothing. A hand groped at the front of her cardigan and his breath steamed hot against her cheek as his big face loomed close.

"You don't have to be lonely . . ." he mumbled.

"Get off!" Abigail turned her face away abruptly to avoid a slobbering kiss. With one violent twisting movement she was free, flinging his arm away from her. "Get away from me and get out of my room, or I'll call the police!"

She backed away and faced him, shaking with fear and disgust. He slouched against the wall and looked back at her, a little warily.

'There's no need to take on like that. I was only trying to be friendly . . ."

"God, you're disgusting! Get out of my room, now!"

He made no move towards her but he was still between her and the door. It would be pointless shouting for help, since there was no one within earshot, as Mr Pearson was well aware. Her eyes darted all over the room for something to use as a weapon, but there was only the wooden chair within reach. She grabbed hold of its back, her hands closing over the spars. If he came at her again she would use it as a shield, like a lion-tamer. But he wasn't a lion, just a grubby middle-aged man with the lechery suddenly gone out of him. He changed his tactic, drawing himself up, straightening his anorak.

"On your high horse, are you? You little . . ." his face jutted towards her, the eyes cold, sneering, "*slut.*"

"Get out," she said between clenched teeth, "and if you dare come near me again I'll report you for assault."

He smiled. "Try that if you like. It's your word against mine, and who's going to listen to you?" He looked her up and down contemptuously. "And remember what I said about the rent. We'll have to review the situation."

"I'll review the situation all right," she said,

anger overcoming fear now that he clearly wasn't going to try to grope her again. "I'll be moving out. You can stick your rent."

He smiled and nodded in a mockery of politeness, and went out, closing the door behind him. Abigail darted across and clicked the lock down, and then stood with her ear pressed to the wood until she heard him go down the stairs and out of the street door. Then she went to the bed and sat down slowly, trembling with fear and outrage. How dare he! How dare he assume . . . ! And she felt ashamed, as if she had actually invited the encounter, or accepted his clumsy embraces. She felt polluted, right through her skin; she could still smell his presence in the room, the sweat and alcohol and stale smoke. She must have a bath, wash the smell away, the contamination of his pawing hands . . . but that meant unlocking the door and going down the corridor to the bathroom, where the lock wasn't completely secure. He had gone out into the street; she had heard him, and he probably wouldn't come back, but suddenly she felt afraid to set foot outside her door, in case he had sneaked back in and was lurking there.

What was she going to do? She had threatened to leave and she couldn't back down. More urgently, she had to get away from that horrible man with his probing eyes and his sweaty hands and his hot panting breath. She didn't want to see him ever again. She kept reliving the way he had looked at her, the way he had suddenly moved in, pawing, slobbering.

She drew up her legs and huddled herself into the bedspread, shivering. Her nose was bunged up, her eyes brimming with tears of anger and frustration. She felt as if she could cry and cry, not only for what had just happened but for the whole hopeless mess she had got herself into. There was no one to help her, no one she could even tell about that awful man, until Gillian came back. The independence she had constructed so painstakingly for herself had been useless; she was alone, vulnerable, desperate.

Everything had gone wrong, everything possible.

New Year's Day 1975

I've only made one resolution. Move out of here.

Abigail had hardly slept, for imagining the door of her room opening. When she did doze, she dreamed of Mr Pearson's big face looming so close that she could see the hairs in his nose and his mouth wet with saliva. In her dreams he became a monster with hot stinking breath and hands upraised like claws. Getting through the night was a major feat of survival.

She got up and dressed, trying to decide what to do. He probably wouldn't try it again, she thought; he had given up quite quickly. If he had really intended to rape her, he wouldn't have been repelled so easily. All the same, she couldn't spend another night here. Anywhere would be better than here, even a shelter on the seafront or under a boat.

Slut, he had called her. She hated the word and he had made it sound even more contemptuous by the way he said it, sneering it. He made it sound like a whore, a prostitute. Is that what he thinks? she wondered. Is that what other people think? More than ever, she felt like hiding herself away from curious eyes, but she would have to go out and find somewhere to stay. In a place like Chilcombe Sands there must be plenty of flats and chalets empty for the winter – there must be *someone* who could help her, let her rent a room of some sort until she could find something permanent. Permanent! Nothing in her life was permanent, not now.

She remembered with a rush of relief that Gillian would be back this afternoon. Without that she would feel like giving up altogether. How *do* you give up? she wondered. Lie down and die? The fact is, you can't give up. As long as you're alive, you've got to keep struggling. Gillian would help her. Gillian would know what to do.

As soon as she was dressed she went out to look for a holiday cottage or flat. Most were shut up for the winter, belonging to people who lived elsewhere. Only once, at a pair of cottages which belonged to a larger house, did a woman come to the door in answer to her knock; she looked Abigail up and down, shook her head without speaking, and closed the door firmly.

By mid-afternoon Abigail was walking along Princeton Terrace hoping that Gillian hadn't decided to come back in the evening, or stay away for another day. She had had no luck, and her only hope now was to ask Bill and Jess if she could sleep on their floor for a night or two. She didn't want to creep back to them in defeat but there was little choice left now. The fluffy white dog yapped at the window as she passed the house next door. If the woman who lived there happened to be looking out of the window too, Abigail thought, she'd no doubt be highly satisfied to see her in her pregnant condition. "In trouble now, aren't you! That's what you get for living in sin!" She could imagine the flushed triumphant face, the smug mouth shaping itself around the taunts. But that was the least of her worries.

It was Max who came to the door. Abigail stared at him helplessly; she had temporarily forgotten that Max lived here too, for all her foolish thoughts about him only a few days ago. He was wearing a baggy Aran sweater and holding a tea-towel.

"Hi, Abby," he said, without surprise. "Come on in. Happy New Year."

She followed him inside, hoping Jess wouldn't be in. But there was no sign of anyone else.

"Is Gillian in?"

"She was, but she went out about twenty minutes ago. We'd only just got in when someone came to the door and Gillian went off with her. She didn't say where she was going or how long she'd be. It was a bit odd, really."

Abigail was disappointed out of all proportion. "I'd better come back later."

"Stay and have a coffee while you're here," Max said. "I was going to make some. She might come back."

"All right. Thanks."

"Sit down and warm up. You look frozen." He pulled a cushion up to the radiator for her and went into the kitchen. The front room still had an unused feel to it, with cardboard boxes stacked in the corners. Abigail wondered whether Max and Gillian spent most of their time together, upstairs; whether they slept together, in the double bed in Max's room. She couldn't imagine them arguing as she and Paul had done, bickering over whose turn it was to go to the launderette or get something to eat. They seemed more grown up – or was it just that she was looking at the relationship from the outside? Everyone had arguments, Granny Alice had said so: it was part of every relationship. Except that not everyone's partner packed up and left when things got difficult. Max wouldn't; Gillian was lucky. Why was I so short-sighted about Paul? Abigail wondered.

Max brought the coffee and sat on the floor near her, clasping long-fingered hands round his mug. He hadn't shaved, and the dark stubble on his jaw made him look untidily attractive, dark-eyed and hollow-cheeked. He looked intently at Abigail and she flushed, wondering whether he had recognized her interest in him at the art exhibition. Regret twinged through her. Not for her the excitement of a new relationship; the only attentions she had received were the pawing hands of Mr Pearson. She felt tainted by last night's episode as if it had marked her visibly.

"Are you all right?" Max asked her seriously.

"Yes – yes, I'm fine." She couldn't tell him about Mr Pearson. It was all too recent and raw.

"When's the baby due?" Max said.

"Oh – around the beginning of June." She

warmed to him for having mentioned it so easily. Gillian must have told him, even if he couldn't see for himself.

"Are you sure you're OK, living there on your own?"

"I don't know. I—" Oh, why wasn't Gillian here? She gulped at her coffee. "Actually no. I wanted to ask if I could sleep here for a couple of nights, till I find somewhere better. Is Jess around?"

"Down at the shop, I think. She won't mind, though. What's the problem at your place?"

"All sorts of things." She avoided meeting his eyes, looking instead at Beano's famous bird of prey painting which was propped on the mantelpiece with a single strand of tinsel draped across the top and a colour postcard marked NORMANDIE propped in front of it. "Did you have a good Christmas?" she asked, trying to be bright and conversational. "When do you go back to college?"

"Fine, thanks. Next week." Max wouldn't be diverted. "Look, I'm sure there's no problem with coming round to stay. You know how easy-going it is here. I'll come round with the car if you like, to fetch your stuff. Gillian's been worried about you living in that bedsit on your own, with no phone – oh, here she is now."

He could see out of the bay window from where he was sitting. The front gate scraped open and shut, and Max looked at Abigail, puzzled. "She's bringing that woman in with her, the one who called. I don't know who she is."

"Oh, damn," Abigail muttered. She wanted to see Gillian on her own. Perhaps the visitor wouldn't stay. Max went into the hall to meet Gillian, and Abigail looked again at the Normandy postcard with the sudden idea that it might be from Paul. She went to the mantelpiece and turned it over, and there was his uneven handwriting, joltingly familiar. *La France is still belle but I'm running out of funds. On my way back to Angleterre for New Year for a bit of sponging*. She replaced it quickly, her mind racing. What did he mean? Was he coming back here? She shouldn't have come; she felt unaccountably disturbed by the suggestion that he was back in the same country, let alone the same town. But Max hadn't said anything about it, and Paul would hardly be anxious to seek her out; he was the one who had run away . . .

She heard Gillian's voice in the hall. "We've been round to Abby's, but she isn't there." And then Max, surprised: "No, I know she isn't. She's here."

He came back into the room, followed first by Gillian and then by Abigail's mother.

* * *

New Year's Day (still)
Everything's changed since this morning.

Mum! Abigail stared, not sure that her senses could be trusted. Mum, here? She leaned giddily against the mantelpiece and gazed at her speechlessly.

A range of expressions flickered over her mother's face. A swift downward glance registered Abigail's changed shape, without surprise (had Gillian already told her?) and then she stepped towards Abigail and embraced her. Abigail's mind reeled. Kay was like a ghost from the past, bringing with her the familiar smells of childhood – her faint perfume, the smell of her old wool coat and the hairspray she used; the same Mum she had always been. But when Kay drew back to look at her, Abigail saw that she was not the same. Her eyes were red-rimmed, her face pale and drawn with tension; she looked smaller and older than Abigail remembered. She gazed at Abigail searchingly and held her by both shoulders as if she didn't know whether to hug her again or shake her like a naughty child in the relief of finding her.

"Mum! How did you—"

"Thank God you're here – oh, it's been so long—"

"But how—"

Kay's voice was unsteady. "Paul didn't know if you were still here."

"*Paul*? Did you say *Paul*? Where is he?" Abigail stared wildly around the room, half-expecting Paul to stroll in.

"I met him. He's at home with his parents. They phoned us last night."

Gillian and Max had tactfully disappeared. Abigail sank to her knees on the floor cushion and Kay sat beside her, one arm round her for support.

"But I don't understand," Abigail said weakly. "Why did Paul's parents phone you? I didn't even know you knew them."

"We contacted them," Kay said, "as soon as you – you left. We knew he was an art student – we got his full name and address from the college records. But his parents said he'd gone to France, so we thought you were there too. Oh, Abby! We had the police looking for you at the ferry ports, the French police too . . . you've no idea what it was like, waiting, waiting . . ."

She pulled out a handkerchief and blew her nose. Abigail groped for her own handkerchief in her sleeve, and unable to find one used the sleeve instead.

" . . . And then it was your eighteenth birthday, and it was out of our hands as far as the police were concerned. We couldn't have brought you back even if we'd known where to find you. You're an adult now . . . All we could do was hope that – one day – you'd come back—" Kay's voice trailed off. Abigail, unable to speak, didn't want her mother to stop talking but hated to hear the awful things she was saying. For the first time Abigail began to glimpse the anguish she had caused.

"And then last night, Paul's parents phoned to say he'd arrived home unexpectedly," Kay continued.

"Why? Why is he at home?"

"Only because he's run out of money, it seems. His parents were so furious with him that they would have kicked him out if it hadn't been for us needing to see him."

"So he told you everything?" Abigail said weakly.

"No. Not everything." Kay's voice hardened. "He only spoke to us because his parents insisted. And he didn't tell us the truth – he said you'd decided to split up. He said he'd expected you to be at home with us. He didn't say anything about disappearing and leaving you to cope . . . or that you're going to have a baby."

Abigail couldn't look at her. "But you did know? Before you saw me?"

"Gillian told me. She was so relieved that I'd turned up. She said she's been worried about you not looking after yourself, not eating well or having proper medical care. – Oh, Abby, why didn't you come home? What did you think we'd do?" It was more of a wail than a question. "Were we so awful? Did we drive you away?"

"No. It wasn't your fault." Abigail found herself concentrating hard on the diagonal pattern of the floorboards. "But I couldn't. I just couldn't. I didn't want you to know."

"I wish you had. I wish you'd felt able to trust us," Kay said wretchedly. She looked at Abigail directly. "Abby, you will come home now, won't you? We do want you back!"

"Why should you, after all I've done?" Abigail said with difficulty. "And . . . what about Dad? Where *is* Dad? Did you come down on your own?"

Kay didn't answer for a moment. I knew it, Abigail thought. Mum might forgive me, but Dad won't. He doesn't want me back. He wants to disown me. And he doesn't even know yet that I'm having a baby. Something hardened inside her, a sense that she had been right to leave home if that was how her father felt. And at the same time she ached with a new hollow of grief, because they had let each other down.

Her mother said unsteadily. "Dad's at home. He couldn't come because . . . we both thought it best if I came. There's such a lot to do at home. Arrangements to make. Abby . . . Granny Alice had a stroke three days ago."

Her voice was so quiet that Abigail knew it must be serious.

"Where is she? In hospital?" Her own voice sounded small and frightened. "Can we go and visit her?"

"No. Not now." Kay looked at her. "She didn't regain consciousness. It was a very severe stroke. She died on Tuesday morning."

Thursday 2 January

We're in a hotel, Mum and me. One of the seafront hotels I've walked past so many times on my way to the harbour. Mum's still asleep – she must have been worn out after driving down yesterday. She didn't sleep well. Neither did I. I heard her muttering and turning over all night long.

We're going home today when we've finished sorting things out. We've got to tell Mrs ABC I won't be working any more. Yesterday we went to Mr Pearson's to give him his key back and tell him I'm going. I didn't tell Mum he'd tried to grope me – she's had enough shocks. But I could tell that Mr P. thought I had, from the creepy expression on his face, all edgy and clammy. Yuck. But that's all in the past now.

I feel so awful about Granny Alice. I'll never see her again. Mum said how horrible it was to see her in the hospital, unconscious and helpless.

Mum knew she was going to die. Granny Alice would have hated to be old and helpless and unable to look after herself – she was so independent. It would have been even worse if she'd survived the stroke and lived on only half there, the way people do. At least this way she was strong and active right up to the stroke. But I wish it had killed her outright. I hate to think of her lying in bed with tubes and things sticking out of her, and poor Mum and Dad waiting for her to die. I've never had anything to do with death, and it terrifies me. How can someone be here one week and gone the next? Where is Granny Alice now?

It sounds stupid but I thought she'd always be there. Whatever else changed, she'd be just the same. Now I'll never talk to her again. I missed my last chance to see her. I wasn't even there in hospital when she was unconscious. Perhaps she knew that. It was my last chance to do something for her and I let her down.

Even worse is the thought that I might have helped cause it. Strokes can be caused by worry, can't they? She must have been just as worried about me as Mum and Dad. Mum said no, she shouldn't think that had anything to do with it, but we'll never know, will we? Granny's gone. I've lost my gran and Mum's lost her mum. Until yesterday she thought she'd lost her mother *and* her daughter.

Now Mum's going to have a grandchild. Granny Alice doesn't know she's going to be a great-grandmother. I think she would have liked the idea.

I'm going home. It doesn't seem like giving in any more. It's no good pretending I can manage on my own. I can't. I need people. And of course I've got to be at the funeral.

Today I'll see Dad. What will he say? Mum phoned him yesterday to say that she'd found me and to tell him about the baby so that he can start getting used to the idea, and not collapse with shock when I walk in.

Today I'll be at home.

"Let's get out of the car," Abigail suggested on an impulse. "Just for a minute."

"But we've only just started," Kay objected.

"Please. I want to have a last look."

The seafront was grey and drab in the cold January light. A recent drizzle had left puddles in the roads and the promenade was deserted, apart from a few gulls squabbling over a fish-and-chip wrapper. The sea, cloud-grey and choppy with white horses, washed monotonously at the shingle, indifferent to human comings and goings. Summer evenings on the beach, with the tide low and the breeze warm from the south, seemed as distant as a dream.

They huddled into their coats and walked down to the pebbles high on the shore. Kay liked it, turning her face into the wind. "I suppose it's a busy place in summer," she remarked. "But it's lovely now. Look at that sweep of the bay, and that wild headland."

Typical Mum. She always preferred holiday places out of season, or bleak windswept heathlands miles from tourists and candyfloss stalls. Abigail didn't tell her that the baby had been conceived by the rocks at the farthest end of the sweep, nor that she had tried to rid herself of it at the wild headland. The place would keep its secrets.

They got back into the car and turned towards the Exeter road. Abigail looked round for her last glimpse of Chilcombe Sands and wondered whether she would ever come back.

Saturday 4 January

We had a long talk yesterday, Mum and Dad and Rachel and me. Mum said that Dad would find it harder than she would to get used to the idea of the baby, and she was right. He went all gruff and funny as if he didn't know what to say. I was glad Rachel was there, really. She didn't treat me as if I've come slinking home in disgrace – well, none of them did. No one's said anything about me leaving in the first place. I ought to have said something, but what? "By the way, I'm sorry I ran away. I didn't mean to." Well, I did mean to, and I can't change that. Knowing how awful it was for them makes me dry up inside. I can't bring myself to say anything about it at all. It's like a big pit, and we're all skirting round it carefully.

But Mum did say something that made me feel awful. Not on purpose, but on the way home I asked what Christmas musical Dad had done this year and she said he didn't do one at all, because he didn't feel up to it. Dad's *always* done a Christmas musical. It's all my fault, but he hasn't said a word to me about making him feel so low.

We're all being very careful not to upset each other, I suppose, because of Granny Alice. There's the funeral to get through. Mum says until that's over she feels she's in suspension. It's awful that immediately someone's died, when you feel worst, you have to make all these arrangements about undertakers, flowers, who to invite, food for them and that sort of thing. I don't think I could cope. It gets in the way of thinking about Gran. We'll have to leave the thinking alone until after the funeral.

Afterwards, when we were on our own, Mum told me she was glad I hadn't rushed off to have an abortion. She told me something about her friend Felicity that she's never told me before, something I'm not to mention. When they were both in the WAAF, Felicity got pregnant and had an abortion in some squalid backstreet place. Abortions were illegal then. It was a bungled job and she couldn't have babies afterwards when she got married. She hadn't told her husband and he had to go through all sorts of tests, when she knew that she was the one who couldn't have babies. It's awfully sad but it made me feel better in a way, because I'm not the only person to get into trouble. You never think of it happening to people Mum's age.

And Mum said she thought I'd been brave. I thought, what an odd thing to say. I haven't been brave, only stupid. But I'm pleased that she said it, especially when I think of all the things she could have said.

It feels so weird to be writing this in my own room. All my things are just as they were – my Paul Simon poster and my books and all the clothes that won't fit me for a long time now. It feels as if someone else used to live here.

I hate thinking that Paul's at his parents' house, not ten miles away. I hope he'll disappear again, and soon. I don't even hate him any more. He's nothing to do with me. He's not

going to be a father, except biologically. It's my life, my baby and my future.

Granny Alice's tabby cat wandered into the hall and back again, sniffing at doorways, occasionally giving a piteous yowl.

"He's all upset, poor thing," Abigail said, stooping carefully to stroke the cat's arched back. "What's going to happen to him?"

"We'll keep him," Charlie said, "now that he's here. He's too old to go to another new home."

"Talking of which," Rachel said, "I suppose you've thought of giving the baby up for adoption?"

They were all in the kitchen, finishing the washing-up and putting-away, with Charlie making coffee. Abigail paused, tea-towel in hand. Rachel had made the remark casually enough, but Abigail guessed from her father's guarded alertness that he and Mum had talked about it between themselves.

"Why?" she said, immediately defensive.

"It's a possibility," Rachel said, "and one you should consider."

Abigail knew it was, although she had never seriously considered it. But had she really thought seriously about anything? Last night, it had been tempting to believe that all her troubles were over now: she was at home, she would be taken care of, she wouldn't have to shiver in a cheerless room or fend off horrible Mr Pearson. But it was time she acknowledged that she wasn't a child any more, running home to report a grazed knee or an unfair punishment at school. Her parents couldn't sort everything out for her.

They went into the sitting-room with their coffee. Charlie said, "Rachel's right, you know. You ought to think very carefully about your future. I don't think you have done, yet. It would solve a lot of problems for you if you did have the baby adopted. There usually aren't enough babies for couples who want to adopt them. It would go to a good home."

"You make it sound like Gran's cat," Abigail said, trying to make a joke of it.

"No, seriously." Kay joined in, sitting forward in her chair. "Have you thought of everything you'll be missing, if you do keep the baby? You're still only eighteen. Other people your age are enjoying their independence – getting jobs or going to college, having the chance for travel, boyfriends, fun . . ."

Abigail shrugged. She already felt years past all that sort of thing.

"Think about it," Rachel said. "You've still got chances. You could finish your college course and find a good job. Have you thought what it'll be like being responsible for a baby?

Looking after it twenty-four hours a day? Not getting a proper night's sleep? Always having to think of it first? Never being able to go out for an evening without arranging a baby-sitter?"

"It means giving up your freedom," Kay said, "accepting that your whole life is going to revolve around the baby. Not just now, but for years and years. You could be – what? middle to late thirties? – before *your* child leaves home."

There was no reproach in her tone, but Abigail guiltily picked up the reference to her furtive departure, and flushed. She was sitting in what had come to be a characteristic posture, one hand resting lightly on the baby-bulge. From time to time she could feel little flickers of movement. Her baby, stirring its limbs. Practising for life. Getting ready to be born.

"It's my baby," she said. "I'm going to keep it."

"Have you thought about Mum and Dad?" Rachel persisted. "Have you thought about whether they want a baby in the house, at their age? They've had their baby years. It'll mean disturbed nights and nappy-changing for them too—"

Kay gave a dismissive gesture. "No, Abby, it's for you to decide."

"As long as you realize what you're taking on, love," Charlie said.

"I have decided."

Abigail heard the stubbornness in her voice. She realized that they could all be forgiven for considering her as stroppy and awkward as ever: refusing to listen to reason, going against their advice for the bloody-minded sake of it. Her own situation was going to affect all of them but they were prepared to adapt, to pitch in and help her, as willingly as if they had chosen it. She was taking that for granted. She tried to explain.

"Everything else I've done has gone wrong. It's my own fault. I've messed it all up. I'm a complete failure." It was the nearest she could get to saying sorry. Charlie began to say something but she held up a hand to make him wait. "Well, this is one thing I'm not going to fail at," she said. "Looking after my baby."

Monday 6 January

Granny's funeral, or rather cremation.

It's going to be awful.

There were so many people at the crematorium. Granny Alice had had a great many friends and acquaintances, and some of them had travelled a long way to be here. There were Kay's cousins from Ireland, relations Abigail hadn't met for years and years – the son and daughters of Alice's twin brother Jack, and Jack's widow who was nearly as old as Alice; even a distant cousin from the Leary branch of the family. There were neighbours, friends and colleagues from the various charities and groups Alice had been involved with. All these people, with Alice as the sole link between them.

"If only she could be here too," Charlie said, "she'd be thrilled to see all these friends and family together."

Perhaps Alice was here, in a way, Abigail thought, in this visible evidence of the connections one person could make.

"I want it to be an appreciation of her life," Kay had said, "more than a grieving for her death. She'd prefer that. Everyone coming together, remembering her. That's how they do it in Ireland. They have a wake, like a big party. A celebration of the person's life."

It sounded a good idea, but Abigail was dismayed when the procession of cars passed between trim beech hedges and she saw the crematorium. Everyone gathered outside the ugly brick chapel and the building adjoining it whose more practical functions were indicated by a tall chimney. Was this Alice's final destination, the full stop at the end of her life? It seemed horribly like being processed, following countless others through this production line. Until Kay had told her otherwise, Abigail had assumed that Alice would be buried by the church at Littlehays, the village where she had lived as a girl. A country churchyard would surely be a more fitting place; Abigail had imagined herself visiting the grave in summer, when the church-yard was lush with wild flowers and loud with birdsong and the hum of bees . . . "No, she wanted to be cremated," Kay had said. "She told me, once. She wouldn't have wanted a church service. She thought it would be hypocritical. She stopped believing in God after the First World War."

Typical of Gran, Abigail thought. So many people put on religiousness for convenience, with their smart clothes, for the sake of having a picturesque christening or wedding, when it was no part of their lives. Not Gran. She had always had strong principles and even after her death she was going to keep to them. Abigail stood apart from the mourners, not feeling up to polite conversation. Charlie, unfamiliarly smart in a dark suit and white shirt, was greeting some newcomers while Kay introduced Uncle Stephen and his wife to some of Gran's London friends. Abigail realized that polite conversation wasn't much to her parents' taste either at present, but it had to be done; hosting a funeral was quite a social obligation. Personal sadness was a private thing, to be kept for afterwards. It occurred to Abigail that she wasn't doing her own duty, by standing apart, and she made her way towards Mrs Richardson, Gran's next-door neighbour, who was looking at her with interest.

"Hello, Abby love. I didn't know you were back at home. Well, you're looking quite – well – not as thin as you used to be . . ."

"Yes, I'm going to have a baby," Abigail said. "Isn't it great?"

"A *baby*! Well!" Mrs Richardson's eyes boggled and Abigail could see the questions *Are you married yet?* and *Who's the father?* hovering unspoken on her lips, together with the condemnatory phrase, *unmarried mother*. Perhaps it hadn't been a good idea to mention it after all, not now, in public; she was wearing her baggy black skirt, hitched up a little for comfort, and Rachel's maroon jacket over it, and no one would be able to tell unless they looked very hard. But then Charlie appeared beside her and linked his arm through hers, and said, "Yes, there's going to be a little Fox. Kay and I are going to be grandparents. Exciting, isn't it?"

Abigail could have hugged hm. He was going to stand by her, and by saying *a little Fox* he had made it clear that she wasn't married and wasn't going to be, and had made that seem unimportant. It was a cause for celebration rather than shame.

"Thanks, Dad," she said, when Mrs Richardson had hurried off to tell someone else.

Charlie looked at her with raised eyebrows. "What for? It *is* exciting. I wasn't making it up. Have you seen Aunt Lorna? She's over there, in the long black coat."

Abigail looked and saw an elderly lady of about eighty, tall but hardly stooped, with iron-grey hair and dark brows, next to a man of about Charlie's age who must be her son. Abigail and Rachel knew her as Aunt Lorna, although she wasn't actually a relation at all; she had been Gran's closest friend for years, and they would have been sisters-in-law if Lorna's brother Edward hadn't been killed in the First World War. Lorna was going to lead the memorial service today, at Kay's request.

"It's better than having the standard formula, from a complete stranger," Charlie whispered. "Lorna will do it well."

It was time to go inside. The undertaker led the way inside the chapel and a sombre silence fell over the guests, all eyes drawn towards the coffin which stood in front of drawn curtains. Abigail sat next to her parents and Rachel, suddenly terrified by the thought that Granny Alice was lying in there, alone and still, and that soon she would pass through the curtains to be consumed by flames. There would be nothing but ashes left. It was horrible, but she knew it was inevitable; and the idea of the coffin being lowered into a grave and covered with earth was no more bearable than this quick consumption. The body in the coffin wasn't Gran. Gran was somewhere else now, and in the memories of the people who had loved her.

Kay stood up first and gave a short tribute to her mother, and then introduced Lorna Sidgwick. Lorna stood up and walked slowly to the front of the rows of pews, leaning on a stick, but there was nothing frail about her voice when she began to talk.

"We are here to give thanks for the life of Alice Leary . . ."

Listening, Abigail realized that her parents had made entirely the right choice in asking Lorna to speak. Lorna talked about the two tragedies in Alice's life and the way she had overcome them, her work as a VAD in the First World War and as an aid worker in the Second, her support for CND and Oxfam since the sixties, her qualities as a friend, companion, mother and grandmother. Abigail saw Lorna as another such, a member of this amazing generation of women who had campaigned for the vote and then lived through two world wars, who had lost their brothers and their lovers in the first war and had then seen it happening all over again; who had worked for a better world in the face of all sorts of personal disasters. Gran had lost her fiancé in the First World War, her husband in the civil strife in Ireland; she had lived in London throughout the Blitz and been knocked over by a police horse at the Vietnam demonstration in Grosvenor Square when she was in her seventies. Abigail felt humbled; what had she ever had to face, in her eighteen years, that matched the momentous events Gran had faced? But her sense of inadequacy was mixed with pride. I'm a descendant, she thought, and my baby will be the next generation. And she felt suddenly certain that her baby would be a girl, a continuation of the direct female line.

In the evening, when all the guests had left and the Irish visitors had gone back to their hotel, Kay said that she was going round to Alice's bungalow, and asked Abigail if she would like to go with her.

"Do you want me to come as well?" Charlie said. "I thought we were going to start sorting things out tomorrow."

"We are," Kay said. "I want to find a couple of things, that's all. You'll come with me, Abby, won't you?"

Charlie said that he would keep Rachel company, and Abigail and her mother went out to the car.

"Do you want to drive?" Kay said, offering the keys.

"No, thanks. Not at night. I'm so out of practice."

The bungalow was in darkness, the windows reflecting the street lights blankly. Always before, Gran had been at home. The thought of the empty rooms struck Abigail more forcefully than anything else that day. Granny Alice was gone.

Kay opened the front door and turned on the lights and drew the curtains. The house was cold but it smelled familiar: odd, Abigail thought, how all houses had their own distinctive smell, nothing you could put a name to, but with her eyes closed she'd know she was in Gran's house. A part of her childhood was disappearing. Gran's house had always been here: a refuge, a place for comfort and warmth and security and fun. Soon it would be an empty shell.

They paused in the front room. The clock that had tick-tocked throughout all her visits was still measuring out time relentlessly, but apart from that it was easy to believe that time was at a standstill, or meaningless. Abigail could see motes of dust hanging in the still air and her own breathing sounded too loud. All Gran's familiar things were there: a pot of dried flowers, a marquetry box with pins in it, a

Wedgwood bowl; a carved wooden donkey bought by Abigail and Rachel on a holiday years ago. Gran's books on the shelves. A calendar standing on the mantelpiece, showing December 1974; Abigail thought of Gran turning over the page at the end of November and looking at the date of her death, not knowing that her own life was running out with the remaining days of the year.

Kay silently led the way into the bedroom. Abigail thought of the last time she had been in this room, when Granny Alice had shown her the paintings. Their last conversation, had they but known it; she could remember everything Gran had said. And I always will, she thought. Patrick Leary looked down from his portrait, sad and introspective, still twenty-nine years old and unmarked by time or grief. Did his spirit survive, somewhere; did he know?

Kay opened the wardrobe door and looked at the clothes inside, the tweeds and wools and plaids at one end, the thinner summer dresses and blouses at the other.

"All her things. I hate to give them away." She touched some of the garments and pulled them towards her and smelled them. "I don't like to think of someone else wearing them, but Mum would hate them to go to waste. I'll have to take them to the Oxfam shop. But I'll choose one or two things to keep."

"Can't you leave it all as it is?"

"No." Kay stooped to straighten a lace mat on the dressing table. "That would make it seem as if we expected her to come back. Sorting her things is a way of accepting that she's gone. Oh, look – here's the bath oil I gave her at Christmas, not even opened."

Abigail stared at it, her eyes filling with tears. *I didn't give her a Christmas present. I didn't even send her a card. The last chance I had.* And she saw that Kay was crying too, and now there was no need to hide it, now that everyone had gone and they were alone. It was an indulgence after the constraints of the day. The funeral had not been as awful an ordeal as Abigail had thought, thanks to Kay's insistence that it should be a thanksgiving, but she was glad that it was over and everyone had gone. She hadn't got used to being back with her family yet.

She blew her nose and stuffed her handkerchief back into her pocket. "What are you going to do with the bungalow when you've cleared it? Rent it out, or sell it?"

Kay looked at her. "I don't know, yet. Dad and I thought perhaps you might like to come and live here."

"Me?"

"You and the baby. When you've got used to each other."

"Gosh, I—" Abigail sat on the bed, not knowing what to say. This could be her home. Not emptied and sold to a stranger, but a home for Granny Alice's great-grandchild. The continuity of it pleased her. She pictured herself playing with the baby in the garden, cooking in Gran's kitchen, sketching by the fire while the baby slept.

"You don't have to make up your mind yet, but it's an idea. Knowing you, you'd prefer to be independent – of course you can stay with us until you feel ready, but it'd be better for you to have a place of your own. And we'll be close enough to help you out when you need it, with baby-sitting and that sort of thing."

"It sounds great," Abigail said. "But haven't you thought of selling it? You and Dad could use the money, surely – have a really special holiday or get some new furniture or something—"

Kay shook her head quickly. "I don't want to think of it in terms of money. This was Mum's home. I'd far rather see you settled. And Mum would have thought the same."

Abigail looked down at the carpet. She wanted to ask, *Are you sure Gran would have felt like that, after I ran away and cut myself off and upset you all so much? What did she think of me then?*

But those questions were too painful to be

asked yet. Her parents were giving her a home, when they needn't have taken her back at all. They still wanted her, even though she had rejected them so dramatically.

"We could start with some redecoration," Kay continued. "You could use the spare room for the baby, but it's a bit dark and dingy in there at the moment."

They went to look at the drab wallpaper and the heavy old-fashioned furniture. Abigail immediately saw the room repainted in fresh colours, with an animal frieze round the wall and a mobile dangling from the ceiling for the baby to look at. "I could even have a friend to stay sometimes," she said, thinking of Gillian. "It'd be terrific, Mum. I don't deserve to be so lucky. Being given a *home*—"

"It's a loan, not a gift," Kay said, "and there's still plenty to think about. For example, what are you going to live on? Are you going to get a job, or finish your college course, and will you be able to find a good child minder? So don't get too carried away."

"But it's a great start. Thanks, Mum."

It sounded ridiculously inadequate. She was being given a home, independence, security, and all she could say was "Thanks".

Kay went back into the main bedroom and stood looking at Patrick Leary's paintings. "It was these I came for. I want to take them home.

Mum left me the self-portrait of my father. All the rest are for me and Charlie jointly, except for the Howth landscape for Rachel. And—"

Abigail's spirits flopped. She didn't leave one to me, she thought. She didn't want me to have one. That means she wouldn't want me to live here either. I'll have to tell Mum and Dad that I can't set up home here; it isn't right, not if Granny Alice wouldn't have wanted it.

"—and *Roisin Dubh*," Kay said, turning to face it, "she left to you."

"Oh, but she can't have done!"

"Why not? She told me she wanted you to have it."

"When?"

"About October, when she told me about her will. She didn't have much else to leave, but she was concerned about them. I joked about it and said she needn't worry for years and years yet, but, well—" Kay seemed to shrink dejectedly into herself. "Odd, wasn't it? As if she knew."

"But *Roisin Dubh!*" Abigail gazed at *Roisin Dubh*'s pale Mona-Lisa-like face, trying to read what she could into the message from her grandmother. It's Patrick's best painting, she thought, the one in which he finally found out what he could do, and Gran wanted me to have it – perhaps because I'm the only one in the family who's interested in art, but perhaps for more than that. She thought of her drawings, which she had carefully packed into a folder. She hadn't mentioned them to her parents yet. "Patrick was right to believe in himself," Gran had said, and, "He was lucky to have found what he wanted to do in life, and to be succeeding at it." Was it a sign for her, that she should persevere with whatever talent she had?

Whichever way she looked at it, she couldn't help seeing it as a sign of faith. Granny Alice had believed in her.

Tuesday 7 January

Today I'm going to help Mum and Dad start sorting out the bungalow.

When I got back last night I took out all my drawings and spread them over the floor in my room. I wanted to see whether I've been kidding myself. Looking at them straight after Patrick's paintings would show them up if they weren't any good.

But I haven't been kidding myself. They *are* good. I showed them to Mum and Dad and Rachel and they all thought so too. I can draw, and I can get better. I owe it to Gran. And to Patrick, in a way – he's thrown me a torch and I've got to keep it alight. I'm not stupid enough to think I'm suddenly going to become a major young talent with exhibitions at the Tate. But – being an artist and bringing up a child – that's two exciting, creative things for me to do. More than enough to be getting on with.

We've sorted out a lot of things. I'm going to join an art evening class, and I'm going to carry on temping. Improve my typing and shorthand as well, because Mum and Dad said that with better qualifications I could get a far more interesting job than the one at dreary old South Devon Insurers.

I keep thinking about Gran. She brought up Mum on her own, without a husband, and things were far tougher for her than they will be for me. If she could do it, so can I.

Suddenly I'm beginning to feel the way they say in the books. I look better, I don't feel tired or sick any more and at the moment I'm bursting with energy. I used to dread feeling like a beached whale but now it's different altogether, as if I'm being carried along on a great strong current, and I don't know exactly where it's going to take me but that only adds to the excitement. Lying in bed last night, I had that weird feeling that everything in my body is working away beautifully and effortlessly to build and strengthen this little curled thing inside me. Sometimes in the middle of the night it seems as if the whole world's waiting.

Waiting for you.

* * *

And now it's your turn. I almost envy you. You're far more likely than I was to make the most of your chances. You're far more mature than I was at your age. I suppose you've had to be, with a father you've never seen and only me for a mother.

I'm so proud of you. You've always known what you wanted to do and now you're going to succeed at it. Is there another Paul out there, waiting for you? If so, you won't fall for him as easily as I did; you're far more cautious. Any relationships you have will be based on equality and respect. You won't be taken in by flattery and smoothness, the way I was.

I've still got the diary I kept throughout those months, although when I look at it now I only notice how much I left out. There are so many things I can't remember without cringing. And yet most of the best things in my life came out of all that muddle – you know that. If I'd been less stupid I wouldn't have you, and that's why I can never seriously wish things had been different. And my closest friends come from that time of my life, Gillian and Max and Claudia. And my painting. I made some painful mistakes, but perhaps making mistakes is what teaches you to be a human being.

One day, if I can bring myself to, I'll tell you all about it.